ALL THE WIND IN THE WORLD

SAMANTHA MABRY

ALGONQUIN 2018

For Kristen D. and her girls

Published by
ALGONQUIN YOUNG READERS
an imprint of Algonquin Books of Chapel Hill
Post Office Box 2225
Chapel Hill, North Carolina 27515-2225

a division of
WORKMAN PUBLISHING
225 Varick Street
New York, New York 10014

First paperback edition, Algonquin Young Readers, October 2018. Originally
published in hardcover by Algonquin Young Readers, October 2017.
Printed in the United States of America.
Published simultaneously in Canada by
Thomas Allen & Son Limited.
Design by Steve Godwin.

LIBRARY OF CONGRESS CATALOGING-IN-PUBLICATION DATA
Names: Mabry, Samantha, author.
Title: All the wind in the world / Samantha Mabry.
Description: First edition. | Chapel Hill, North Carolina :
Algonquin Young Readers, 2017. | Summary: Working in the maguey
fields of the Southwest, Sarah Jac and James are in love but forced to
start over on a ranch that is possibly cursed where the delicate
balance in their relationship begins to give way.

Identifiers: LCCN 2017020570 | ISBN 9781616206666 (hardcover)
Subjects: | CYAC: Ranch life—Southwestern States—Fiction. |
Secrets—Fiction. | Love—Fiction. | Southwestern States—Fiction. |
LCGFT: Thrillers (Fiction)
Classification: LCC PZ7.1.M244 Al 2017 | DDC [Fic]—dc23
LC record available at https://lccn.loc.gov/2017020570

ISBN 978-1-61620-855-4 (PB)

10 9 8 7 6 5 4 3 2 1

First Paperback Edition

"Won't you lend your lungs to me? Mine are collapsing."
—Townes Van Zandt

PART ONE

THE COUSINS

ONE

THE GOAL IS to get to the heart:

Slash off the spines.

Sever the bulb from the roots.

Move down the row.

There are other steps to the maguey harvest, but I'm responsible for only those three. There are men who drive the trucks, and there are kids who jump down from the beds of those trucks to load up the hearts, which, once shorn of their spines, are the color of milk and roughly the size and shape of medicine balls. The hearts are then taken to factories by train, where they're roasted and mashed until they produce a heavy, smoky-sweet liquid. That liquid, when distilled, becomes pulque, mescal, or, if you are rich, tequila as clear as a tear.

It's morning. I'm on my way to the fields when I hear a whistle from a passing train. The sound hits the mountains and hums a ragged tune across the plain. We tell time by whistles:

3

7:10 in the morning westbound, 9:22 in the morning east-bound, 2:20 in the afternoon westbound. We know it takes ten minutes at a steady run to the south-southeast to get to those tracks from camp. We've timed it.

The truck I'm riding in starts to slow and pulls alongside several others just like it, all crammed with workers. We clutch the long handles of our coas, hop down from the truck, and take our places in front of a row of spiky plants that seem to disappear in either direction into the orange-hued horizon.

A gust of wind comes through, carrying with it a strange smell: something like sulfur mixed with citrus fruit.

"I'm surprised how late you slept, Sarah."

My heart lurches, then yanks itself back into place. James has snuck up behind me enough times in my life that he shouldn't cause this kind of reaction, yet somehow he still does. I turn to see him standing no more than a foot away, his eyes glinting, much like the blade of his coa does in the desert sun. I can tell he's worried about me, just on the edge of frustrated. When he gets this way—which is often enough—the brilliant, moss-green color of his eyes comes out.

"No, you're not," I reply.

"I thought maybe you wouldn't make it out."

"No." I flash James a grin. "You didn't."

We're surrounded by other jimadors, so we're talking in code. I'd rather we not be talking at all. I'd rather it be like last night late, when it was just the two of us on the outskirts of camp, out in the scrub grass under the harvest moon, when the only sounds coming from James' mouth were the syllables of my name broken by sighs.

"No," James says. "I didn't." He glances at my blade.

As usual, I woke up late, and, as a result, am stuck with a dull tool.

"The sun's not even all the way up, but it looks like you've already run out of luck for the day," he says. "I'll trade you if you want."

"*Please*," I scoff. "I could cut more maguey than you with a butter knife."

James laughs, which is wonderful. He does this automatic thing where he lowers his head and covers his mouth with his hand, like he's embarrassed. He *is* embarrassed. There's a scar at the left edge of his upper lip, the result of a dog biting him when he was a kid, way before we met. Whenever he laughs or smiles wide, his lip tugs up a little bit, like it's being sewn with a needle. It's hardly anything, but to James it's conspicuous.

Sometimes I think that there's so much sameness in the desert. The bunkhouses are the same peanut-shell color as the dirt. The dirt is the same color as the mountains. Most days, the sky is striking in its clear blue, but there are few birds that fly through it, and the ones that do are black. Our long days are reiterations of the long days that came before. It's tough to tell young from old or man from woman because the desert has a way of erasing the things that make us each unique. Flying grit scrapes away at our faces. The wind tries to knock us flat, and the sun tries to bleach us, dry us out, and turn us into dust.

All the wind and dirt; it doesn't scrape away at James. It polishes him to a shine. He's alive out here. He stands taller. His eyes shine brighter.

I lean forward, as if to dive into those eyes. He leans forward, pretending to examine the nicks on my coa blade.

We've done a version of this thousands of times: hovering whisper-close to each other. But each time the feeling is new and thrilling, like snatching something from a store shelf or trying to outrun the rain.

Another whistle blows—this one just near my right ear and most certainly not from a train—and James and I fly apart just as one of the foremen jerks his chestnut-brown mare to a stop alongside us.

"James Holt," the foreman barks. "You think you and your cousin get paid to stand here and admire the weather?"

James snorts. "What's biting you, Angus? New horse causing you trouble?"

It *is* a new horse, a sorrel I've never seen before. She's twitchy, obviously uneasy. She tosses her head, her nostrils flaring as she sniffs the sulfur-tinted air. She shuffles forward, then back. Angus responds by gripping the reins and pulling hard. The horse squeals as the bit pulls against her gums.

"You're too rough with her," I say.

"Too rough?" Angus yanks again. The horse squeals, then stills long enough for the foreman to lean down and level his eyes with mine. "You haven't seen how rough I can get with the girls who piss me off." He grins, revealing a jagged row of gray teeth. "Now get moving."

I END UP working alongside a wisp of a man who showed up at camp a couple of days ago with a little kid who coughs a lot and is probably consumptive. The boy may be his son, but I doubt it. The kid has his arm in a splint made of burlap and wood. Because of that, he can't cut crops or work mess, so he sits on the ground between the rows of maguey attempting to make small houses out of the discarded spines, which is nearly impossible because the wind that's come in strong over the course of the morning keeps knocking them down. He reminds me of my sister, Lane. This is exactly something she would have done at that age: create castles out of trash and never get discouraged when something comes around and knocks them down. There was no such thing as a lost cause to that girl.

For the last hour, the man has been carrying on a mostly one-sided conversation with me through the dusty red bandanna that covers his nose and mouth. His voice is muffled, but I've gathered that he's from California, where there are still grapes.

"Have you ever eaten a grape?" he asks.

The man goes on to tell me that he wants to leave the maguey fields and go out East and into some other line of work. He says he's pretty good with numbers and could be a book-keeper. He tells me he's got a bad leg, points to a visibly swollen knee, and says he won't be able to continue to do physical labor for much longer.

"Where were you before here?" I ask. "Ojai?"

The man shakes his head. "The Real Marvelous. It's a ranch in Texas, just outside Valentine."

"I hate to tell you this, but if you're trying to go east you're headed the wrong way. This is New Mexico."

The man stops cutting, takes a dirty piece of cloth out of his back pocket, and wipes his brow. A sudden, sharp gust of wind knocks into him, and he's forced to check his balance. He winces, clutching his knee. "You're trying to be cute," he growls, "so obviously you know nothing about that place."

I shrug. "I know a little—from the people who've passed through. It's big, bigger than here. The pay isn't all that great, but at least there's always work there."

"There's always work there because no one *wants* to work there." The man leans in and lowers his voice. I can smell the sharp tang of his breath. "Those fields are cursed. The owner puts hexes on the workers and . . . *stuff* in the food to control us. This knee." He gestures to his leg. "This is not a normal injury. It's punishment. I got together with some of the other jimadors and asked for better pay. Not much more, just a few measly cents. I don't remember hurting my leg at all, but then, one morning I wake up . . ." The man trails off, hitching his eyebrow and assuming I can fill in the rest.

My gaze catches on the bundle of sticks and dried herbs that hangs around his neck as a common, crude protection against harm. A superstitious jimador like him would wear it under his shirt at all times, nestled against his breastbone, right in front of his heart.

Some people out here believe in all kinds of shit: cursed fields, gray-skinned demons that rise from the cracks of the earth, jackals that come out during full moons and walk around on just their hind legs, or a jumble of sticks and twine that somehow magically keeps bad things at bay.

"Interesting," I mutter.

The man shoves his cloth back into his pocket and starts cutting again. "What about you and your cousin? Is this the only ranch you've worked on?"

"It's the third," I reply.

"Where else?"

"The first was outside Tulsa. Then one a ways north of here, near Picuris."

"Neither of you have parents?"

"Not anymore."

"Well, I'm sorry to hear that." The man sighs and glances over at his boy. "Where are you two headed next? Surely you don't want to go on cutting maguey forever."

I look down the row at James. Even with the hard gusts of wind and dust blowing in his face, he's working at twice my speed. He's strong. His muscles have memorized this work. Mine have, too, but James is different. He has this focus. He cuts the plants like they're his enemy, but he's calm about it. He never stops working to wipe the sweat and dirt from his eyes.

He says he doesn't really think about the sun or discomfort when he's cutting. He thinks about other things.

When I ask James what "other things" he thinks about he just smiles that ragged, brilliant smile of his.

James and I could work in these fields, doing the same thing every day, for the rest of our lives. More than half the continent is desert now, from the Mississippi River to the Pacific. Much of the South has started to dry up, too, or so I've heard. Maguey grows quickly in the dry climate, and water is scarce and not to be trusted. Much of what's left is salty, unfiltered, and full of the dust-remains of dead fish and birds. Alcohol, like mescal or pulque, on the other hand, is clean and safe; it burns away impurities.

Ranches like this one, just outside Truth or Consequences, New Mexico, are the new lifeblood of the country. Here there are hundreds of hectares of fields reaching past the train tracks and toward the mountains. These fields provide the raw material that will lead to millions of gallons of alcohol. James and I could hop trains, moving from ranch to ranch, following the harvest, always smelling like dried sweat and feeling sticky from maguey sap, for years, decades even, until our bodies give out. We've seen it happen: older men or women, their muscles cramped into angles, their skin baked to their bones, stop cutting and just . . . sit. No amount of shouting from the foremen or pleading from the other jimadors will make them move. Eventually, they're hauled up by their armpits and tossed in the back of a truck with the maguey hearts. We don't see them again. The foremen tell us they are taken, along with the milk-white hearts that have piled up like severed heads, to the factories, and that they work there, in relative comfort, indoors and out of the sun. I don't know if this is true. There's no telling where those people go. The desert is a big place.

This is not our plan—to be old bones in the desert. Our plan involves saving up enough money so that we can catch a train that takes us far away from these fields, all the way to the East Coast, where James and I can open our own ranch, not for cutting maguey but for breaking horses. We'll go and dip our feet into cold ocean water whenever we want. We're young; we still have time. We work smart. We work fast.

I hear the man beside me grunt, so I turn to face him. He's stopped cutting again and now has his foot braced against the side of a maguey plant. His coa blade is stuck in the heart, and he's attempting to dislodge it by wiggling the handle side to side as if trying to free a loose tooth. A combination of the wind and shifting his weight to his bad leg causes him to fall to the earth and let out a muffled curse.

I set down my tool and go over to grip his. With a cut this deep, the plant is ruined, so I work to save the tool. The wood starts to strain as I push on the handle, and I think for a moment it'll snap. I throw all my weight into it anyway, and the blade pops free, accompanied by a sucking sound. A fist-sized hunk of the maguey heart soars through the air in a short arc and lands at my feet.

I help the man to stand and hand him back his coa.

"If you cut too deep like that," I say, "you'll destroy the heart. You want to use your blade like it's a paring knife, and you're trying to slice the orange part off an orange. No more."

"I know how to cut maguey," he mutters.

I don't get the chance to reply because some jimadors farther down the row have started shouting.

"Down!" I hear them cry out. *"Get down!"*

I turn slowly, my stomach dropping, and see the storm: a hazy, rust-colored curtain extending from the ground to the sky. Its roar is a dull moan now, but it's building fast. Within seconds, it'll crash down on all of us.

One after another, the jimadors drop to their knees, bracing their coas against their bodies and the ground because a loose coa in a dust storm is a bad thing. My own tool—the one that I'd dropped in order to help the man with his stuck blade—starts to skitter across the dirt. I lunge forward and barely get my fingers around the handle before it spins away. Then I press my lips together and angle my face away just as I'm pummeled by a hard mass of grit and wind.

This is protocol: make your body small. Cover your nose and mouth. Don't lose your blade. Wait.

I fold forward and into myself, pressing my forehead to my knees. I start to hum a song, an old one my grandmother used to sing to me and Lane at bedtime when we were little and there were lightning storms. Sometimes, if I'm able to create a vibration in my head, I can drown out the wind and distract myself from the fact that I can't breathe.

Here's another thing some of the jimadors believe: a dust storm is made up of the scattered, unsettled fragments of the past that insist on never being forgotten, like some hateful phantom. When they finally arrive, those fragments plow into you, burrow into the folds of your clothing, and stick in the spaces between your teeth. They want to be a part of you. They won't let you go.

Other people claim the opposite, that because a dust storm pops up so quickly and seemingly out of nowhere, it serves as a reminder of the unpredictability of the future. It represents uncertainty, total chaos, or, worst of all, futility.

I don't believe any of this, but I'm still terrified. My humming isn't working, but I keep it up anyway. I can hear the man next to me calling out to his boy, telling him not to panic. The boy is crying. I hear him say he can't breathe just before the hiss of wind heightens into a terrible, all-encompassing roar.

Seconds pass, maybe a minute. Then, over the wind and the hum in my head, I hear a horse. Its hooves are hammering against the ground. It's snorting and screaming.

The rider has no control. He's shrieking his commands. I lift my head a fraction and see that it's Angus. His sorrel is snapping her teeth and spitting, and even through the dust I can see the whites of her panicked eyes. She's near—maybe just thirty yards away and closing fast—and if she doesn't stop or change course, she'll plow straight into the man from the Real Marvelous and his boy, who both have their heads down and are huddled against each other.

I push myself to standing. The wind immediately catches my coa and knocks me off balance. I'm pretty sure I can hear James calling out to me from several yards away, but I ignore him. I know my way around a horse, and I don't need his help with this.

I lurch forward and wave the blunt end of my tool in the direction of the horse's flaring nostrils. My intention is to get her to circle around, run back the other way, but instead she comes to a halt, screeches, and then rises up on her hind legs. Her front hooves thrash at the air. A good rider will know what to do in a situation like this, but Angus has never been a good rider. I slam the blade of my coa deep into the ground and lunge for the horse's reins.

"Get back!" Angus yells.

I ignore him. If I can just grab hold of the reins, I can get the horse to turn.

"Get back, you stupid bitch!"

Just as my fingers find the leather, Angus kicks out, and the steel toe of his boot crashes into my left cheek. My head rings, chiming like when someone smashes down on a bunch of piano keys at once. I tilt back, my vision, for an instant, white, but I've somehow managed to keep my grip on the reins.

"I can help!" I cry out.

The horse lands, her hooves slamming down just inches from my feet. She twists and screams, backs away, and then rears up again.

"I don't need your fucking help!" Angus shouts.

The leather strap finally rips out of my hands. I grit my teeth and shove the horse.

From there, the wind takes over, slamming into the both of us. I fall instantly, sideways like a felled tree, but for a moment, the sorrel is suspended motionless, nearly vertical. Then, slowly, she begins to tilt and tip farther until her back legs buckle underneath her and she plummets to the ground. She twists in the dirt before jerking herself upright and thundering away, her saddle half-stripped from her body. I look to the man from the Real Marvelous, the one I was trying to help, and through the orange haze of dust, I see him clutching his boy and glaring at me as if I've brought the devil down upon us all.

My gaze tracks over to Angus. His wide eyes are frozen toward the dust-choked sky, and his limbs and head are at odd angles. There's a bone, oddly white, sticking out from his shoulder. His hand is the closest thing to me, palm facing up, like he's giving me a gift.

I sense vaguely that James has his arm around my waist and is trying to get me to stand. He's saying something, but I can't understand what.

There's a break in the wind, just brief enough for me to hear the sound of men shouting, whistles blowing, and more horses approaching.

I'm standing, and James is tugging at my wrist. I understand now that we have to run. We have to run because I made a mistake.

TWO

THE 9:22 EASTBOUND train is tearing across the desert in front of us. It should've taken us ten minutes to reach these tracks, but it feels like at least double that because the dust has been steering us in circles, and we've been straining against a thick wind determined to throw us back to camp. It was only when we heard the train blow its whistle that we knew for sure which way to run.

The storm is starting to die out, and I can now see the last train car down the tracks in the not-so-distant distance. There's a good chance we'll miss our opportunity to jump on. If that happens, we'll either suffer heat death out here or be hunted down and taken back to camp, where our executions will be made into a public spectacle. Ranch owners don't look kindly on the death of one of their foremen, even if that death was technically an accident. I'd prefer the heatstroke because at least then I'd die at the hands of the elements and not at those of some jefe.

I'm running on pure fear right now. I've always thought I was the weak link in our chain and that I would eventually bring James down with me because of some dumb thing I said or did.

James bolts ahead. With one final push, he takes a running leap and grabs the metal handle of the door to the open train compartment with both hands. The toes of his boots skid across the dirt for a couple of yards before he's able to pull himself up and into the cargo car. He catches his balance, wipes his hand on his jeans, and reaches out to me. I run faster because he's getting farther away and smaller, and I can't bear the thought of him being carried away with one arm extended toward me like this.

James knows if I push I can reach him. The long strands of muscle in my legs feel like they're about to rip, but I manage to catch up to the train and sprint alongside it. The roar is incessant, deafening. Heat rushes up from where the steel wheels meet the track. It reeks like rust and burning metal.

I jump. Our fingertips flutter against one another for the briefest instant and then slip away. I lose my balance, find it again, and charge on. I time my steps, find a rhythm, and jump again. My hand grips his. He shifts his weight back and pulls me toward him. My legs feel suddenly heavy, then suddenly light. I'm up off the earth, letting out a strangled cry and soaring. My spine wrenches, then slams against the floor of the car. My chest heaves, and I start wheezing as I stare up at the rusted roof of the empty train compartment.

I stay like this for only a couple seconds before I push myself up to a seated position, scoot myself back against the side of the car, and put my head between my knees. I can breathe better now, but my heart still thrums in my ears. My legs are so used to running, they won't stop twitching. A knot's forming in my right calf. I wince and flex my foot in the attempt to release it.

"Here." James digs into one of his pockets and pulls out two strips of jerky wrapped in a damp cloth. "You don't want cramps." He offers me both strips, but I only take one.

"I'm sorry." It's all I can say.

Our money, everything we'd saved from our work in the fields is sewn into my mattress in a bunkhouse I'll never see again. I've never lost this much before, only a couple bucks that were stolen from underneath my pillow by some girl back when we first started cutting maguey.

"I have some," he says. "A dollar and some change. I picked it up this morning before you were awake."

Several days a week, James gets—*used* to get—a small group of itchy men and boys together to throw dice against the wall of the mess building before the fires got built and the foremen came out with their dogs and their horses. Angus would join in. James always said he was the perfect gambler, which meant the young foreman talked an enormous amount of shit but never learned when to stop throwing down coin.

They weren't friends by any stretch, but James and Angus had a mutual agreement that seemed to work well. Angus would look the other way on the games as long as he was allowed to play every once in a while. When he was feeling generous, James even let Angus win a game or two.

"You said you'd stop." My remark is halfhearted. Normally, I'd be upset with him for being careless with his money, but obviously circumstances have changed.

James reaches out and intertwines his fingers with mine. He rubs the calloused surface of his thumb over the lines of my grime-streaked palm. He's a good person, certainly too good for me. Ever since I met James two years, four months, and eighteen days ago, he's been essential to my survival, and I sometimes really hate myself for that.

"You would've acted differently," I say.

His response is immediate. "Probably."

James is studying my palm, and won't look me in the eye. He wants to say more, possibly read me the riot act—we both know I've earned it—but that's all he'll give me right now: a *probably*. Somehow that one word seems like the worst of all the things he could say.

I swallow some more of the jerky, which does nothing but cause my stomach to kick and remind me of how thirsty I am and how we have no water. It's not even midmorning. It'll be hot soon, and we'll bake in this metal box for hours. Then, after the sun sets, we'll freeze. This is the way of the high desert. It goes from one extreme to the other. I'm almost too exhausted to care.

James scoots in closer, but still doesn't raise his head. He smells like sweat and smoke and dirt and engine oil, which is how he always smells. I lean into him and rest my head against his chest. He wraps one arm around me, which makes me feel a little bit forgiven.

James eases his fingers into my matted hair, and I close my eyes. I'll fall asleep this way—propped up against James—for the first time in months, and I'll probably sleep for hours and hours.

IT's DARK WHEN we're both rattled awake by a pounding above our heads. Our limbs untangle, and we launch apart. James jumps to his feet. On reflex, he reaches down for the bone-handled knife he keeps in the lining of his boot. I stay in a crouch. When I breathe I see the vapor escape between my lips.

The sound above us travels the length of the train car and stops. I stand as a head-shaped shadow drops into the open doorway. Whoever it is scans our empty cargo car from an upside-down vantage point, sees us, pauses, then vanishes.

"Hey!" James shouts. There's a croak in his voice. "Do you have water? We'll trade you gold for water."

The head reappears, a dark mass against the sky. I can't see James' hand, but I imagine his knuckles are nearly as white as the bone of his knife handle. We don't know if this person is a stowaway like us or a thief who rides the trains to prey on stowaways, but both James and I are so wracked with thirst we have to take the risk.

"What do you have?" From the close-cropped hair and tenor of the voice, I assume it's a guy our age, or slightly older.

"Jewelry," James replies. "Worked gold and silver."

"Let me see," the guy demands.

"Let's see the water," James fires back.

The head grunts and vanishes again. I reach to my waistband and pull out a once-white, now dun-colored bandanna I keep tucked against my skin. It holds several pieces of jewelry—bracelets, charms, and pendants—most of which are stolen and I'll part with for next to nothing. There's one piece, though, a thin, rose-gold necklace that belonged to Lane. That one I'll keep forever.

The contents of my bandanna and the few things James keeps stashed away in the pockets of his pants are all we have left. My hand trembles as I shift through my jewelry, and my legs are shaky beneath me. My quivering muscles and James' raspy voice tell me how much we desperately need water. The physical need is one thing, but the panic of being parched in the desert is worse.

"Hard hearts," I whisper as a reminder to both of us not to show weakness in front of others.

"Hard hearts," he echoes.

Within seconds, the guy reappears, waving a waterskin. I approach him slowly, holding one end of a delicate chain of gold between my thumb and middle finger. The bracelet sways with the motion of the train. The guy studies it briefly.

"Deal," he says, tossing me the waterskin.

I pass over the chain and drink, ignoring how the warm water in my empty stomach makes me nauseous. When I'm done, I toss the waterskin to James, who takes a more meager pull.

The guy doesn't wait for an invitation before gripping the top of the train compartment with both his hands and flipping into our car. He lands on his feet in front of me, revealing his towering height. Not at all fazed by the five-inch blade James is holding in plain sight, the guy hides the gold away in the depths of his cargo jacket and smiles, revealing a chip in one of his front teeth.

"I'm Leo," he says as he takes back his waterskin. His breath smells like mescal. I'd know that smoke-tang anywhere.

"I'm Sarah Jac. This is James."

Leo steps around me and takes a cross-legged seat in the center of the car.

"Make yourself at home," I say.

Leo grins. "You two just hop on?"

James nods.

"Jimadors?"

"Yeah," I reply.

"Me too," Leo says. "Lucky for you. At this point, we're only a little over a day away. I've been on this train for almost a week. Since Salton City. It's gotten to the point where I'm so bored I can't even fall asleep. Has that ever happened to you? It might be the moon, so low and bright like it is—like this giant eye staring right at me. So where are you two from? Like, where are you *from* from. Your accent, it reminds me of someone I used to know. You're not from the South, that's for sure. I'm originally from Oregon, but I got out of there pretty quick."

James tucks his knife back into his boot and glances over at me. We're thinking the same thing: this guy sure is chatty. He must be telling the truth about being a jimador. If he were a thief, the amount of wind coming out of his mouth would've gotten him killed a long time ago.

"We're from Chicago," James offers.

"That's it," Leo says, clucking his tongue and wagging his finger. "I once knew a guy from Chicago. He died."

I don't say anything because that doesn't surprise me in the least.

Leo tells us we're a long way from home, as if that wasn't obvious, and I don't say anything to that, either. It's uncomfortably quiet for a while, and he eventually takes the hint.

"Well." Leo unwinds his long legs, rises to stand, and starts digging around in his pockets. "I guess I'll leave you two lovebirds alone."

I don't freeze up, or blush, or look away because I've come to expect people to say something along those lines when they first meet James and me. I laugh, though, and so does James, but in this very specific, very grating sort of way that only I know is fake. It's aggravating how good he is at this: pretending he's embarrassed of me or, worse, that he finds me repellent.

"Actually," James says. "Sarah Jac's my cousin."

"Oh," Leo replies, still rummaging around in his pockets. "Okay. Well . . ."

"You never told us where this train is headed," I say. "You just said we're a day away. A day away from what?"

"The Real Marvelous." Leo glances up. "In Texas. I thought you knew that."

I tense. Leo doesn't notice, but James does, of course. His gaze flickers across my face.

Finally, Leo finds what he's been searching for. He takes out a bracelet—the one I just gave him—and holds it out. "I'd be a total jerk if I made two thirsty cousins pay for water." He steps forward, leans in a little, and smirks. As Leo drops the chain into my open palm, I smell the liquor on his breath again. "Just don't tell anyone else about my kind and gentle nature, alright?"

"How many?" I ask.

Leo raises an eyebrow, taken off guard by my ill-mannered reaction to what he obviously intended to be a generous gesture. "How many what?"

"How many jimadors are on this train?"

"Maybe forty," Leo replies, heading back over to the open door. "Give or take."

"Thanks for the water," James remembers to say, nudging me in the ribs.

"Yeah," I mutter. "Thanks for the water."

Leo shrugs like it's no big deal, hops up to grab the top of the compartment, and flips up the reverse of how he came in. James and I wait until we can no longer hear the sound of his boots stomping over our heads before turning to face each other.

"What was that?" James asks. "At this point, we need all the friends we can get. Leo said the name of that place, and you went cold."

"Sorry. It's nothing." I shake my head. "Just that man I was working with earlier today mentioned something about it. The Real Marvelous. No one wants to work there because the fields are cursed and the owner puts hexes on the workers."

James snorts. "Since when do you believe in hexes?"

"I don't."

I cross my arms over my chest and gaze out into a dark night lit by a low, bright moon. Leo was right—it looks like a great big eye staring right at me. But there's no magic out there, I remind myself, no spirits rising from the split earth, just fields upon fields, slamming into mountains, and maguey in those fields, waiting to be cut, waiting to be turned into money in my pocket.

"We could stay on the train," James offers. "If that's what you're thinking. See where it takes us."

That's not what I'm thinking. I don't know what I'm thinking. Out in the distance something catches my eye. It's a solitary deer. I can just see its outline and its glassy eye reflecting the moonlight. James sees it, too—a large, wild land animal is not a common sight here. Most have been pushed north and east by the heat and the cold and the lack of water. What's left of them have been hunted down for food. The deer takes a tender step forward, stops. Its ear twitches and then rotates. It hears something we don't and then darts away.

"I was scared today. When that horse was charging toward you . . ." James trails off, and I know what he's doing: replaying the event in his head, re-splicing its frames, fixing it.

"We've had some close calls before," I say. "Outside Tulsa was worse."

"I'm tired of close calls, Sarah," James replies. "I'm tired of this life, the ruse, putting you into these types of situations . . ."

"You didn't put me into any situation. This is what we do together. We hop trains, work fields, save money."

James takes a step back, shaking his head. After Lane died, I was incapable of making any kind of decision. I was dead weight that James practically had to drag from Chicago.

"I don't want to have to lie anymore." His voice has gone brittle.

That worry, that frustration from earlier this morning is back, and I can hardly blame him for it.

"That's all we do out here, Sarah. If we keep telling each other to have hard hearts, then we're going to have hard hearts. Is that what you want? To end up like some of these workers, or these foremen, who've turned into monsters with human skin?"

"James." I reach out to him, but he doesn't take my hand. "I'm not . . . I was trying to do something good. I was trying to save those people."

"And then you were trying to hurt that foreman. I saw you push his horse."

"I didn't mean for him to die! The wind came and . . ."

James says nothing, but there's an ugly twitch at the corner of his lips.

"You're disgusted with me," I say.

James clucks. "Of course I'm not *disgusted* with you, Sarah. But you have to realize there are things you can't fix. You can't just stand in the way of fate and wave your arms hoping it'll turn the other way."

We're silent for a while, the both of us thinking. He said there are things I can't fix, and while that may be true, there is one thing I *can* fix. I pivot toward James and tell him: this is what we'll do. We'll get off the train. We'll work harder at the Real Marvelous than at any place we've worked before. Forget hexes. Forget poison. We're stronger than all that. We'll cut so much maguey, piles and piles of it. After six months, no matter what, we'll go east, toward the ocean, where we'll ride our horses and pick fruit off trees and dive into cold breaking waves.

"How does that sound?" I ask. I can't fault James for being beat-down and skeptical right now, but I need to know that he still believes in us.

James smiles, just a little. I will take that little smile as a gift. I will.

WE SPEND THE next day going over our plans for the future because that's what we do when we need to pass the time and can't work with our hands. James' mood has lifted since yesterday, so he starts. He says that he'll find us a deserted island off the Eastern Seaboard. He'll find a hill on that island, hollow it out, and that's where we'll live, underground like weasels. There'll be no windows, just a little wooden door and a chimney. Inside will be an iron cookstove, a bed with a handmade quilt, a rocking chair, a fireplace, and a table. The wind may batter our hill from time to time, but we won't ever notice.

When it's nice out we'll walk for miles and swim in the ocean—even at night. When the weather's bad, we'll stay inside and make up stories with us as the characters.

"But we can't be the good guys in all of them!" James shouts as he stands halfway out the door of the train car, balancing on one leg, allowing the wind to yank at his hair and his clothes. "Sometimes we'll have to be the bad guys."

"Of course," I reply. "I'll be the evil genius, and you'll be my sidekick!"

"Perfect!" he shouts back.

I'm okay with our house built into the hill as long as I can have my horses. I'll pick a favorite and call her Daisy. She'll be mine, but only because she wants to be. I won't stable her or anything, but she'll come around some mornings and let me saddle her, and we'll run laps around the island. I'll whoop into the sky knowing that no one will ever hear me.

There's one more thing James wants our island to have, something that will make it perfect: a big tree with a whole mess of branches, all bursting with green leaves. He wants a tree so tall that when he climbs into its highest, most tender limbs, he'll feel weightless, like the winds are always threatening to shake him loose. He'll defy those winds and climb higher.

This is the very best plan.

Just before the sun sets, Leo stops by with more water, jerky, and dried figs. He's sort of drunk again, and as he's taking a piss off the side of the train, he launches into a story about his last stint cutting maguey out near Salton City. The overseer there went crazy one day, started screaming about fantasmas, and took swipes at the workers with a coa. One guy tried to stop him and got whacked in the neck and died. Another got three of his fingers sliced off. Finally, a group of jimadors tackled the overseer and held him until the other foremen could drag him off. After that, the field was labeled cursed, and most of the workers—including Leo—left to catch the next train headed east.

"Not that I really believe in all that stuff," Leo says. "Ghosts and shit like that? But—let me tell you—once those rumors start, about curses? Camps clear out *fast*."

James and I share a glance.

Leo goes on to tell us his dream of saving up enough money to buy a parcel of land in northern Mexico. He wants to get rich running his own maguey fields. He wants a big house—a house made of *bricks*, he says—and a cellar full of wines with names he can't pronounce and a bedroom with thick red curtains that block out the sun so he can sleep as late as he wants.

"Forget the East!" Leo leans farther out the side of the train, letting the wind tear at his face. "Too cold! It's so beautiful out here. I'll be so happy to be buried in this ground."

"We miss water," James replies.

When we lived together in Chicago, James and I had our lake. It, too, was in the process of drying up, but still, it was something. But as I study the passing landscape, I have to agree with Leo. It *is* beautiful out here, in its own way. I love the hot days, the hard expanse of ground, the little lizards that hide in the creosote, the imposing mountains, the way the wind, when it hits the right speed, sounds like a string section playing in a minor key. It's dangerous out here. I've warmed up to that danger. I still want my house in the hill, but I'm hot-blooded now, too.

ON THIS NIGHT, our last like this for a while, James and I curl up together in the corner of our cold train car. He rubs my arm, trying to create warmth, and I nuzzle my nose into the crook of his neck. I inhale deeply and feel the goose bumps ripple across his skin.

"What are you doing?" James asks, pulling me closer.

"Smelling you," I mumble.

James' laugh rumbles in his chest. "Why would you want to do that?"

"I like the way you smell." I breathe in. "Like smoke and dust." I breathe in again. "And engine oil."

"I haven't worked with machines in months." James' voice is low and quiet, like he's almost asleep. "How can I still smell like engine oil?"

"You just do. Back when we met you smelled like engines, so that's how you'll always smell." I shift, crawl on top of him, bringing my lips to hover over his. "Do I have a smell?"

"Yes," James replies automatically.

It thrills me that he knows this, that he's thought of it before.

His eyes are closed, but he grins slightly. "You have a definite smell."

"Which would be . . . ?"

James' smile grows wider. He won't cover it when it's just the two of us. "Gamey."

I try to jerk away, but James holds me in place.

"I smell like *meat*?"

He opens his eyes. "You smell like *you*. Like campfires and spice. Like a wild animal."

I'll take that.

"How about . . ." I start to say. "How about . . . I'll give you my smell, if you give me yours?"

James closes his eyes again. His grin still lingers. He's waiting for me to kiss him, and I do. I kiss him and inhale him at the same time, knitting his scent and the sure, soft urgency of his lips into my memory.

A deep growl rises from the back of his throat, followed by all the syllables that make up my name: "Sarah Jacqueline."

I work to keep this memory, too: the way he says my full name when we're alone together, how it's gruff with wanting, how he takes his time to unwrap it like a present, unroll it like a banner, or open it up like the pages of a Bible.

THREE

THE NEXT MORNING as the sun breaks, we all launch ourselves from the train and run toward the maguey fields of the Real Marvelous. We run because in most camps not everyone who wants a job can have one. There are only so many beds and supplies an owner can provide. We also run because, after all that time stuck in the train, it feels good to be using our bodies again. We whoop and shout, and the sound shoots across the desert.

People new to this part of the country sometimes describe it as barren, but that's just them not looking hard enough. Under the cracked surface, the fire ants swarm in a cool, dark empire. Lizards and rattlesnakes emerge from the depths to warm themselves on hot rocks for the day. The birds here—every last one of them black with oil-slick feathers—don't fly so much as soar in perpetual circles, watching and waiting. The creatures that live out here are smart and resilient; they have good instincts; they know when to strike and when to rest. I tell myself that I should be more like them. There is sameness here in the desert, yes, but there are also treasures.

News must have traveled about a train full of jimadors coming this way, because a foreman is waiting for us at the camp gate. He's like a version of St. Peter dressed in gray and black and wearing mirrored sunglasses. I'm the first to reach him, and the others line up behind me. The foreman doesn't even give me time to catch my breath before gripping my arms to feel for muscles and spinning me around to lift the back of my shirt to check the straightness of my spine. He scans my eyes for the yellowing in the whites that's common with disease.

"Have you cut maguey before?" he asks.

"Yes."

"How many plants can you down in a day?"

"As many as you need me to."

The foreman grunts in approval and waves me through. Inside the gate, another man points me toward the women's bathhouse.

I look back and see that James is also waved through—of course—and sent in the other direction. It feels strange for us to part after so much time together, but I can still pull his scent from my hair and my clothes. He gave me his; I gave him mine.

The woman working in the bathhouse finishes the drag she's taking off her hand-rolled cigarette and tells me to strip. After she inspects my clothes and hair for lice, I'm allowed to shower. She hands me back my bundle of clothes, and after hanging them on a hook, I head over to the closest water spigot. The meager lump of soap provided is black, made of lye and coal. The water's not exactly hot, and the whole place smells like old milk and seems as if it's coated in layers of slime, but I don't know when I'll be able to feel water on my skin again, so I make the most of it. After washing and rinsing, careful to leave enough soap for the women who've come in behind me, I duck my head under the spray. It's good to feel clean.

I turn off the tap just as a woman comes in holding the hand of a whimpering little girl. They remind me of the jimador and his boy back at Truth or Consequences and how my soft heart cost me a good thing. I won't let anything like that happen again. I cross over to where my clothes are hanging, and since there don't appear to be any towels, I dry off with my dirty shirt.

After changing back into my clothes and checking to make sure I still have my bandanna and my jewelry, I step outside to view a flat expanse of rose-gold dirt dotted by maguey plants. Over to the west, there's a ragged line of mountains.

I weave through the rows of bunkhouses and spot the owner's house, atop a far, wide hill several hundred yards away. It's a sprawling thing, a single-story structure surrounded by a five-foot adobe wall. A red-and-white flag waves lazily from a pole in a courtyard. There's a twisty gold symbol in the middle of it, like several snakes all tied up in a knot—maybe the crest of the owner's family. To the left of the house are some tidy stables and an exercise yard for horses. There's a girl there, reed-thin and almost ghostly, leading a large white horse by the reins.

The wind shifts so suddenly, it nearly knocks me off my feet, and brings with it the smell of roasted meat coming from camp. Like a starving dog, I turn on instinct and see a growing number of freshly inspected jimadors all congregating in a large common area between the bunkhouses near a pit, where some of the young mess crew, the ones responsible for preparing our food and cleaning up after meals, are flipping thin strips of meat over a coal fire.

I remember what the man back at Truth or Consequences said, something about things not being right with the food, how the owner put *stuff* in it. I scan the crowd and find James. Our eyes lock. His brow hitches up, just slightly. I'm ravenous, so I'm willing to take the risk. I make my way into and through the line, get my plate of food, and take a seat on the ground near the fire. Then I dig into the meager bits of charred, fatty meat with my fingers. James takes a seat beside me, and together we eat in silence, waiting for the overseer to address us.

I've seen pictures in books of men all tied up together, wearing striped clothes and breaking rocks with sledgehammers on the side of the highway. Chain gangs, they used to be called. In those pictures, there's always one guy off to the side, wearing dark pants, a shiny, saucer-sized belt buckle, and a white button-up shirt, with a rifle slung over his shoulder and a couple of dogs at his feet. The overseer of the Real Marvelous ranch looks like that, as if he studied those pictures to get the details just right.

"Newcomers!" he calls out. "Welcome to Valentine, Texas. We call this ranch the Real Marvelous. Here's what you all can expect."

His dogs—a duo of muscle-bound mastiffs the blue-black color of true night—sit on either side of him and grunt as their master explains the rules.

"Breakfast starts at six thirty. We leave for the fields by seven. There's a fifteen-minute break at eleven. We stop at three. By five, the harvest for the day is totaled, and you are paid according to the amount you cut—five cents a plant—minus your room and board, the cost of water, and the cost of the diesel fuel it takes to cart you all out into the fields."

I do the math. That leaves us with anything from thirty to thirty-eight cents a day per man. The wage isn't much. Some of the jimadors grumble, but no one gets up to leave and wait for the next train to come through. I crack my knuckles. I can't wait to get a blade in my hand again and start working.

The overseer begins to say something about how they issue coas here, but stops and glances over his shoulder as a man on horseback approaches. I know immediately who he is. Unlike the rest of the men in charge dressed in blacks and smoke grays, he's in a suit of lightest brown. His clothes are too clean and fit too well, and his skin is too pale for him not to be rich. He's the owner, a rare sight. They don't usually want to see us, and we don't want to see them. I'm sure this man spends most of his days inside his comfortable house up there on the hill, balancing his ledger books, admiring his horses, listening to his flag flap in the wind, and sipping silver tequila from glasses that aren't flecked with chips.

He rides up next to the overseer and leans down from the

saddle. The two men talk briefly, and the overseer steps back to give the owner space to address us.

"Welcome again." The owner's voice booms. "Be aware, you're joining near on two hundred other jimadors already here, and you'll have to prove your worth in order to stay. I expect everyone to do his or her job here, and do it well. Idleness will get you sent out to jump the next train. Those who cause trouble will be punished first *and then* get sent out to hop the next train. I'll see to that punishment myself."

A girl next to me snickers, causing her friend to jab her in the ribs.

I fight back my own smile. The owner's trying to assert his authority, which I suppose is fine, but I've never been afraid of a ranch owner, and I'm not about to start. I look over to James. He's glaring at me. His hard frown wipes the smile right off my face.

My gaze drops down to my empty plate, and even though I just finished eating, my stomach pops with hunger.

IT'S HOURS AFTER supper and most of the jimadors have retired to their bunks, but, still, it takes James no time to get a game together. All he had to do was pull his old deck from his back pocket, sit down in a clearing near the edge of camp, and start to shuffle. Leo sidles up, bringing with him some other people from the train. Most of them are from Salton City, but some have come to Valentine from such far-flung places as Idaho and the Dakotas.

I'm worried that they can all smell Angus' death on me, but to my relief, no one tells a story about a dust storm and a dead foreman in Truth or Consequences, yet they all have stories, and similar ones: foremen going crazy from the heat, taking off all their clothes and dancing in the field; foremen getting caught having sex with the jimadors; foremen getting caught having sex with the livestock; foremen getting drunk and killing other foremen. Most everyone is laughing—though not loud enough to draw attention from the night guards—but I watch a young couple, Ben and Rosa, who've come from Arizona, as they eye each other. There's string peeking out from the collars of their shirts and the slight bulge of fabric in front of their hearts. They're wearing those bundles of sticks and dried herbs around their necks. Madness in the fields isn't funny to them.

"I left Joshua Tree because the maguey started bleeding," a girl named Odette tells us. She has corn silk hair that spills down her back and large, round eyes that give her a slightly stunned expression.

Leo snickers, pulls a flask from his shirt pocket, and takes a pull.

"I'm serious," she says, chewing on a fingernail. "I struck my first plant one morning, and blood so dark it was almost black came oozing out. It was all over my coa blade. I couldn't wipe it off."

We're all quiet for a moment. Ben pulls Rosa into his lap. She drapes her arm around his shoulder and starts to run her fingers through the loose curls at the back of his neck.

Bruno, a big, brawny guy who told us he's been at camp for close to six months, glances over at them. His eyes narrow slightly before he turns his attention back to the cigarette he's rolling. It's odd for a couple to lay claim to each other that way, to show such open affection. It's a clear invitation for people to start talking.

The firelight flickers against Bruno's large hands, and I can't help but admire the careful work he's doing. The delicate rolling paper is crisp and uncreased. The tobacco is spread out perfectly.

"We've all seen things we wish we hadn't," James says.

Odette lifts her head and offers James a wobbly smile. She doesn't know that even though he's looking at her, he's not talking to her. He's talking to me. Like he always is.

James calls that hand a wash, shuffles a new one, ups the ante, and just like that restores the mood. We play for what seems like hours in good spirits under a bright-eye moon. James' original ante of a dollar has doubled. Others are winning too because James is letting them, especially Odette, whose trembling fingers and open face betray every hand she's dealt.

"I love it out here," Leo eventually says. He gestures out toward the horizon and grins his messy grin.

It's late, but there's still a strip of peach at the bottom edge of the sky. Out West, the days hang on this way. They cling to the crust of the earth. This is what Leo must be talking about: it's admirable, the way the day refuses to give up, the way it always wages a battle against the oncoming night.

But I'm wrong. That's not what Leo's talking about at all.

"All the lies," he says. "The desert seems so simple and boring, but really it's full of secrets. When the Spanish first came here all those hundreds of years ago, they had no idea what to make of it, so they just started coming up with lies."

"Call," James says, ignoring Leo, who is—no surprise—a bit drunk.

As Bruno lights his cigarette with a match and I toss down nickels, Leo throws down his cards and leans forward to draw a small X in the dirt between his feet.

"Did you know that Cabeza de Vaca was, like, right here?" Leo asks, pointing to the ground. "Did you know he told the Indians that he was a healer? He said they wouldn't get sick ever again if they just became Catholics. He also said that when he was lost for weeks, the thing that saved him was a burning bush." He laughs, too loudly, and waits for a reaction that never comes.

"A *burning bush*?" Leo urges. "*Like Moses?* He saw a burning bush *like Moses*. And there were other people, too—telling lies that went across this country, across the ocean to Spain, up into the stars, and even deep down into this dirt." Leo swipes his hand through the air, side to side, up and down.

I can't help but laugh. He looks like a terrible, lazy wizard trying to conjure a spell.

"You think this is funny, Sarah Jac?" he asks.

"I think it's really funny."

Leo shrugs. "Fine. But I'm right. That's what happened with Odette over there. Her and her bleeding maguey. There were all

se lies in the ground that got sucked up into the roots of the
nt. She freed them with her blade."

I show my hand. It's a winning straight.

"I thought you didn't believe in stuff like that." I bend over
collect my winnings. "Ghosts and curses and shit."

"I don't believe in *curses*," Leo says, rising to stand. He takes
a step forward and looms over me. "But I believe in lies. And
liars."

His eyes are very clear, not dull and unfocused like I'd expect
them to be since he's been taking pulls from his flask all night.
Leo's revealing himself to be tricky, hard to read. I can't tell if
he's trying to threaten me or let me in on a secret. I have enough
secrets of my own. I don't need any of his.

"You're a very philosophical drunk, you know," I hear James say.

"And quite the historian," Bruno adds.

"I'm right," Leo replies, swaying like a reed in the wind.
"You'll see."

ONCE WE'RE FINALLY alone, huddled shoulder to shoulder
in the cold, James and I count our winnings: four dollars and
fifteen cents.

"Just enough for ice skating and cocoa," James says with a
smile.

He's right. For the three of us—me, him, and Lane—to go
skating on the frozen pond in Chicago and have cups of hot
cocoa, it cost exactly four dollars and fifteen cents.

I love James for remembering this thing I forgot. I love the

41

quiet thrill he gets in his eye when he knows he'll win a ha[r]
love him, my partner.

So I surprise myself when I say, "Odette's the one."

James' smile twitches, then vanishes. He dips his head. "[S]
a possibility. But I was also thinking that maybe we don't [
to do it this time. The others here, they seem alright."

I'm silent, and James knows what this silence means. I disagree. *Hard hearts.* He might not always like it, but it's true. In our world, you hide your bruises; you don't let people know you have weak spots. It's like asking for trouble. Everyone knows two people in love will do anything—stupid things—to save each other. And everyone, no matter how *alright* they initially seem, will take advantage of that.

"She's pretty," I say.

"She's gullible," James shoots back. "It helps that she looks nothing like you."

"Helps with what?"

"Your jealousy. I don't want to be your cousin, Sarah. And I don't want to come on to some poor girl who thinks that a maguey cactus can bleed. I don't want to be with her when I could be with you."

I'm conflicted. I think back to my grandmother: what would she say if she were here with me under this big moon, a fugitive fleeing one field to hide in another? She was goodhearted like James, but she was also crafty, a tactician. She had her rules, good rules, that she would remind my sister and me of when

I sigh and look—not to the mountains, but to James. He's filthy. His hair is all mucked up, standing on end. There's a grimy smear across his forehead and what appears to be a small, crusted-over cut near his ear.

He smiles—just barely. "They look like they're dusted with copper."

Finally, I turn to face the mountains, and, yes, that's exactly how they look: dusted with copper. Shimmering and beckoning. Glowing in the sun. My grandmother once told me about how people in the past flocked to mountains like these to search for gold. They rarely found it. Most of them drove themselves crazy with desire and died, but I can't blame them for believing this land was bursting with treasure. Treasure, not lies.

"You finished?" James gestures to my water cup.

He takes it from me just as the foremen start blowing their whistles, signaling time to get back to work. His fingertips brush against mine but don't linger.

ABOUT AN HOUR after our short lunch break, the sky darkens. The wind changes direction, gets stronger and cooler, and out in the western sky, charcoal-colored clouds above the mountain range start to blink with lightning.

This sliver of time without full-on sun is when the owner comes out to survey his fields. He's on his white horse again and accompanied by his overseer and a girl about my age I assume is his daughter. If I had to guess, I'd say she's the same girl—willowy and pale—who I saw yesterday out near the house. They bring their horses to a stop several yards down the row as one of the foremen approaches them. He points to specific workers and then gestures grandly out to vast fields. This is the owner's treasure: not gold bursting from mountains but healthy maguey plants bursting from the earth. The owner nods often. The girl does nothing. The overseer's two mastiffs, both the color of the storm clouds over our heads, have come along as well. They lie down in the dirt and pant. One barks. It sounds like a steel door slamming shut.

The wind that's been torturing me all morning proves to be only a minor inconvenience to the girl. She sits tall in the saddle, never angling her cheek away from the grit that flies in her face. She doesn't wear a hat because she won't be out here long enough to need one. The wind gently catches her hair, the color of which matches the dusty copper of the mountains. She's dressed in riding clothes: a crisp, chalk-white shirt, black pants, and knee-high black boots. If she were closer, I'd be able to see her eyes shining with pride, a different kind of pride than the one I feel after cutting maguey all morning. Mine is a pride earned; hers is pride easily received, as if she'd held out her open palm during a storm and then took credit when a raindrop fell to the center of it.

Her horse is gorgeous, an even better animal than her father's white stallion. It's the color of over-milked tea. Its mane and tail are matte black. There's a mark on its hindquarters, a white circle the size of a dinner plate. The horse kicks impatiently at the ground. I wonder if it's fully broken and how fast it can run. Pretty fast, I'll bet.

When the four of them—the foreman, the overseer, the owner, and his copper-haired daughter—start to make their way down my row, I strike the maguey with the force and precision of a worker whose arm muscles haven't started twitching from fatigue. For the sake of both my pride and my pocketbook, I hope they notice my skill and the quality of my work, but when they pass behind me, they're speaking a proper dialect of Spanish I've never been able to pick up, so I have no idea if it's me they're talking about.

Suddenly, I hear one of the horses squeal, and just like that I'm taken back to the dust storm at Truth or Consequences. My heart flies up into my throat as I spin around and see the girl's horse twist and stutter-step out of the row and right into the sharp spines of a maguey. I look to the sky. It's dark, but there's no dust. The brown horse squeals again. On the ground there's a rattlesnake uncurling just a couple feet away from the horse's front hooves. It must have burrowed under a maguey as the clouds came in, and now it's angry about being disturbed.

I expect the well-bred daughter to scream, or at least yelp, but she's composed as she tries to calm her nervous horse. The snake slides forward, eyeing a strip of muscle on the horse's thin front leg. It shakes its rattle and opens its jaws to snap. I rush forward, bring down my coa, and, with one clean swipe, sever the snake's head. Stepping over the still-twitching body, I grab the horse by her bridle. She tries to toss her head away, but I hold firm.

"Shhh, girl." I kick the snake's head away. "You're fine. See? I killed it."

I don't want to look at the girl, so I keep my focus on the horse. She's calming, but it's obvious she's young. There's a wildness in her eyes.

"Your horse needs more breaking," I say. "It's not good when they're so skittish."

"Thank you, young lady," the owner says, cutting in. "We'll be on our way."

A moment passes. I nod, releasing the horse and stepping back so that the owner and his daughter can continue past. Finally, I pull my gaze up and note how unruffled the girl still seems. She lifts her chin, just slightly. This is the tiniest bit of recognition and gratitude she can spare. That gesture is honestly more than I expected.

Before turning back to my work, I glance over and notice that James is trying to stifle a grin. I can't help but smile as well.

See? I want to say. *See how helpful I can be?*

WE'RE AT THE end of our afternoon water break when Odette pulls me aside. She lays her tool in the bed of one of the trucks so she can take both my hands in hers, interlacing our fingers as if we're childhood friends.

48

"So," she says, pinning me with those big, saucer-shaped eyes. "Your cousin . . ."

Odette casts a cautious glance over her shoulder to where James is leaning against his coa, talking to some other workers. Just then the foremen start blowing their whistles, signaling us to get back to work.

Odette doesn't let go of my hands, but instead squeezes them harder. Her grip is strong, but I can still feel her trembling. "He was so kind to me, and . . ." She falters. "I mean . . . Can you give me any advice? Any way that I might go about trying to . . . you *know*?"

Yes, I *know*—because this has happened before, in other camps. She wants James to want her.

For the briefest instant, I regret suggesting Odette as the one. Maybe we can find another. Most girls who've lived this life, in fields and on trains, are either tough as leather or free as air. Odette, though, is thin and brittle to the point of breaking. I can feel it in the way her hands are shaking. I can see it in the way hope and desperation flicker in her eyes.

"I think that you . . ." I give Odette's hands a squeeze. She'll think it's to reassure her, but really, it's just to buy me time to find the right response. "I think you should just . . . just . . . go for it. He's always liked girls who know what they want."

Odette exhales, softens. "Thank you, Sarah Jac. I really appreciate it."

The foremen blow their whistles again. Odette drops my

hands and grabs her coa from the truck bed. As soon as she turns away, I look to James. He's not smiling anymore. His frustration hits me like a wall of wind.

Dinner is quiet, only some halfhearted chatting around a halfheartedly built campfire. Most of the jimadors rush to shovel down their undersalted beans and stale cornbread and head to their bunks before the chill of night sets in. From my seat on a wooden bench near the dwindling fire, I watch as James approaches, holding his plate. He takes a seat next to me and angles his legs slightly to one side; our thighs don't touch.

"How much did you make today?" he asks.

"Forty-eight cents."

He's impressed. I can tell by the little clucking sound he makes in the back of his throat.

"Did you see Leo at all?" he asks.

I didn't, and I'm surprised I didn't. If Leo was in the fields, I'm sure I would've noticed. He's mouthy and tall and kind of hard to miss.

James motions with his head as he stuffs a piece of cornbread in his mouth. Leo is at the end of the mess line, waiting to get his dinner. Even from yards away, I can see that his eye is prune-colored and swollen shut. There's a gash across his eyebrow.

"Were you there for the fight?" I ask.

James shakes his head and swallows his food. "It must've been late last night after we'd already gone back to the bunkhouse."

Dustups at camp are common, and in the short time that

we've known him, Leo has proven to be both loose-lipped and a sloppy drunk. So it wasn't Leo getting into a fight that surprised me. "Even injured, they would've made him work," I say. "Back in Truth or Consequences, they made that one lady cut maguey with a broken hand."

"They did," James replies. "They did make him work. Just not in the fields. He's working with the horses up at the ranch house. Apparently, he has experience with that kind of thing."

How James would've learned that Leo got a job working at the house so quickly, I have no idea. But that's beside the point. James knows I'd shovel shit all day if it meant I could be near those horses.

"Speak of the devil," he says.

Leo approaches carrying a dented pewter bowl full of food. Up close, his eye looks even worse, swollen and wonky as if the socket's been busted.

"I fell," he says, shoveling a spoonful of grayish beans into his mouth.

"Naturally," James replies.

"So you work with the horses?" I ask. "I saw a couple in the field this afternoon."

Leo's eye twitches as if it's painful to chew. "With Gonzales and Farrah?"

I nod, filing those names away.

"I heard about what happened with you and the rattler," Leo says. "That new horse, the brown one, it's young and nervy, and apparently has a habit of getting loose and running away." He pauses. "Listen, my face hurts like mad. Do either of you have any pulque?"

"No, sorry," James says. "What was Gonzales doing out there?"

Leo shakes his head and goes in for another spoonful. "Admiring his bountiful crops, most likely. Can you blame him? Seriously, you two don't have any alcohol at all?"

I don't answer. I'm staring into the fire thinking about how glorious it must be to work with horses all day, to brush their coarse hair and lead them in laps around the practice yard. Out of the corner of my eye, I can see James draining what's left of his water. He stands, tells Leo, "Let's go find you something to numb that pain," and pats me on the shoulder. It's a gesture so lacking in intimacy that it spoils my daydream.

"See you in the morning, Sarah Jac," he says.

As the two of them head off, I hear Odette call out James' name. Both James and Leo turn at the sound and then head in her direction.

I wonder if James will take Odette to some corner of camp tonight. Will he get tipsy and kiss her the moment they find themselves alone? Or will he sit with her for a while, thumbing the strands of her long corn silk hair, telling her fake stories about the fake adventures that he and I spent night after night making up together? She won't know those stories are fake. She'll be so won over by him. She already *is* so won over by him.

The whole time he's with her, he'll be thinking about me.

He'll be thinking, *We're such tricksters, Sarah. I told you we can't be the good guys all the time.*

I stay where I am and keep staring at the campfire, but since no one is tending it, the logs all collapse onto one another and turn to smoking embers within minutes. The sun hasn't even fully set yet, but this day feels long. I stand, and, after handing off my dishes to the kids in the mess crew, I make my way back to the bunkhouse and fall asleep faceup on my cot.

A dream about my grandmother using pliers to fix the gaps in her wire fence shifts into a nightmare about me suffocating during a dust storm. Just as I'm taking what I'm sure is my last gasping breath, I'm jolted awake. Someone has their hand clamped down over my mouth.

FIVE

ON A WELL-HONED instinct, my hand clenches into a fist, and I swing. Whoever's there catches my wrist with their free hand and pins it down beside my head. I try to yank free, but am held firm. I inhale—sharply—and that's when I know my attacker isn't an attacker. He smells too much like engines and dust.

It's James. His face is hovering just above mine. He's smiling, holding back a laugh, so he obviously isn't here to give me bad news.

One of his hands still covers my mouth. I rake my teeth across his rough palm and bite down just hard enough to make him wince. He releases me, puts his finger to his lips, and then motions with his head: *Come with me.*

It's cold, so we move quickly, skirting behind the bunk-houses toward the south side of camp, where the supply sheds and the mess buildings are. The moon gives off just enough light for me to see the clouds of James' breath against the night sky. Our hands are clasped together so that James can lead without losing me.

Voices rise up from the direction where the fire was earlier. They belong to men who either can't or refuse to go to sleep, but those men are far enough away and most likely drunk enough that we don't have to worry about them noticing us.

We reach the mess building, and James comes to a stop.

"You scared me to death," I whisper. "What is it?"

James spins around and points to his ear: *Listen.* I hear snorting, heavy breathing. Stifling a gasp, I reach out and grip James' arm. Together, we creep around the rear of the building, and there she is: Farrah Gonzales' tea-brown horse, munching on scrub grass.

She senses our presence and whips her head up. Her wide, glossy eyes reveal distrust, as do the muscles rippling down the length of her body. I slow my breathing to slow my heart rate to try to prove to her I'm not a threat.

"It's just me," I say. "I heard you're a handful."

The horse shakes her head, snorts, and goes back to eating.

"I couldn't sleep," James says. "I was roaming around when I found her and then came to get you."

I hold out my hand, palm up, and click my tongue. The horse isn't completely sure about me, but still, she stretches her neck forward. Her breath is warm. I wait for her, and after a few seconds, she tilts her graceful head and nuzzles it against my palm.

"She's great," James says. "When Leo said she had a rebellious streak, it reminded me of someone else I know."

All this time, my other hand has been holding James'. I only now notice because it's only now that he releases it. He steps away and leans against the side of the building.

"What's wrong?" I ask.

"Are you alright?" James sighs. I hear him crack his knuckles. "I mean, with Angus. You haven't said much about it."

I focus on the point of contact between my hand and this beautiful animal, my rough skin against the horse's coarse coat. It's warm there, full of life and comfort. "Sometimes when the wind kicks up, I feel this flutter of panic. And then I look around and wonder who's going to be next. Like I'm expecting to make some dumb mistake, and someone will die because of it."

"I'm sorry I suggested it was your fault," James says. "It wasn't."

"It *was*. You were right."

For a while James says nothing, and then: "The feeling, that panicky flutter. It may never go away. It might just have to be something you learn to live with."

I nod, biting the inside of my cheek.

"I had a nightmare," James goes on to say. "About Lane. It woke me up, and I couldn't go back to sleep."

My hand falls from the horse's face, and I turn. James is all shadows in the black night.

"That hasn't happened in a while." I reach for James again, and he pulls me toward him. I make myself heavy, and we click into place. We both need comfort tonight. "Odette's falling for you," I say. "She told me in the fields."

"She's not the one I want," James murmurs into my hair. He drags the tips of his strong fingers across the line of my jaw, laying claim. "You're the one I want. You're always the one I want."

I grip James' shirt, and he brings his mouth to mine. Just as his tongue grazes the seam of my lips, I hear it: the crunch of a boot, followed by another. Someone's creeping around, trying to be quiet.

I start to pull away, but James holds me tight.

"It doesn't matter," he whispers, his voice gruff.

I hesitate, just for a moment, before stepping back. It's dark enough that I'm spared the sight of James' expression, but I see him lower his head and rake his hands through his hair.

"Britain!" a low male voice calls out. "Britain! Here girl."

James' eyes flash up to mine, and his jaw tightens.

From around the side of the mess building comes the bobbing stream of light from a handheld torch.

Leo, James mouths.

Sure enough, the torchlight bends, and around the building comes Leo's lanky figure. The leather lengths of reins and a bridle are looped around his shoulder. The unexpected sight of us nearly causes him to drop his lamp.

"Shit, you scared me! What are you two doing out here?"

James tells Leo what he told me: about not being able to sleep, taking a walk, finding the horse, coming to get me.

"Her name is Britain?" I ask.

"Yeah." Leo works to secure the horse. "Sorry I always catch you two at a bad time."

"No worries," James replies. "Sarah Jac and I were just out here hatching our magnificent plan to take over the ranch."

Leo laughs. "Don't forget to include me, alright? Since I work in the house, I know all the secrets. Isn't that right, girl?" He strokes Britain's nose. "See you two later."

We say our good-byes, and James and I wait until we can no longer hear the soft clicks of Britain's hooves hitting the earth. I realize now my hands are shaking. I shove them into my pockets, grateful that the cold weather gives good cover for my jangled nerves.

"That's twice now he's snuck up on us," I say.

James says nothing; the steam of his breath rises up and disappears into the air.

"I don't trust him," I add.

"You don't trust anybody."

"Since when is that a bad thing? James, he's taunting us. He *knows*. You know he knows."

James squares his shoulders. "So what if he does?"

"You aren't serious," I hiss. "What do you mean *so what*? I don't have to stand here and tell you what he could do. He could—he could blackmail us. He could turn us in to the foremen, and *they* could blackmail us. He could try and turn us against each other." I step back and let out a breath. "It's like you've forgotten about what happened in Tulsa."

James lets out a long, low whistle. He can't believe I brought up Tulsa, given that I know how much he wants to wipe that place from his memory. Tulsa was where we went after we left

Chicago. This was back before we pretended to be cousins, back when I sat in James' lap around the bonfire like Rosa did with Ben and he rubbed my sore shoulders. We openly adored each other, and it nearly got us both killed.

"Of course I haven't forgotten about what happened in Tulsa, Sarah." James takes a step back and throws up his hands. "You know what? You want me to go after Odette? Fine. I will. It'll be the best acting job you've ever seen."

"James . . ."

I hear a train blow its whistle, from the south I think. I have no idea how far away it is; sound can travel in tricky ways.

"Just know that the whole thing will be over *the second* you say it's over."

He waits for me to respond, to tell him that's not what I want anymore, but I don't.

"Okay?" he says. "Hard hearts, right?"

I worry that my heart is not very hard anymore. It's getting tired and worn out, like maybe its fibers are coming undone. After Tulsa, we started scheming. James blames himself for what happened there; I blame me. We're both still trying to make it right by doing things that feel wrong, like pouring more lies into this lie-soaked land and duping poor superstitious girls.

But I don't want to tell him that. I've already said too much—about Angus, and about the wind making me nervous. So, instead I say, "Right. Exactly. Hard hearts."

James lets out a sigh. He's disappointed, but still, he pulls me into an embrace. I tangle my limbs with his and crush our bodies together, like we're both going into battle with weak armor and are pretty sure neither of us will return.

THE NEXT DAY, I think it's the end of the line for James and me. That we're done for. Thirty minutes into the morning's harvest, a pickup pulls to a stop in the row behind me. The driver says, *Hey, girl,* and tells me to get in back. I freeze mid-strike. My tool hovers above my head. It's the first time I've been called out individually, and I assume it's because I match the description of a girl who killed a foreman one state over.

I twist my coa blade so it glints in the sunlight. I wonder if slicing the truck's rubber tires will buy me enough time to run to the train tracks. The driver is a paunchy, gray-haired man with a days-old cigar clenched between his teeth—no match for me unless he has a pistol stashed in the glove box. Now that I think about it, there's a good chance he has a pistol stashed in the glove box.

I scan the field for James before remembering that he went out to work in a different one this morning. That means running isn't an option. I won't leave without him.

I look back to the driver. He picks a speck of tobacco from his lower lip and then flicks it at my feet. He repeats his command in Spanish. When I still don't reply, he asks, "Are you stupid or something?" He leans farther out the window, extends his arm, points at me then to the bed of the truck. *"Let's move, perra."*

After a short ride that feels much longer, the truck pulls up to the ranch house and parks next to the yard where the horses are kept. The owner's white horse is nearby, munching alfalfa. Britain is standing at the opposite edge of the enclosure, surveying the desert expanse and swishing her tail. Both are fresh and saddled.

Leo emerges from the stables, greeting me with a chip-toothed grin that somehow makes his face even more grotesque. A black scab divides his bottom lip; purple bruises on his cheek and around his eye have faded to the color of mucus. His smile widens, but I'm not encouraged.

Behind him come Farrah and a younger version of Farrah. The younger one has the same shimmery copper hair but is half-sized and plumper. They are both dressed in tan riding pants and white button-up shirts. They grip their black helmets down by their right hips. Unlike Leo, neither of them is smiling. Instead, as they walk toward the horses, they both hold their heads at a tilt, slightly up and to the left, like they're trying to peer up and over my head and to the mountains beyond me.

The little one looks to be about how old Lane was when she died, maybe a little younger. Her chubby face tells me she's full of health and cake. I hate her instantly.

"Sarah Jac!" Leo approaches the truck and extends his hand to help me down. I don't take it and step out on my own. He shrugs his bony shoulders before heading over to a wood gate that leads into the courtyard surrounding the main house. He motions for me to follow. I stay rooted.

"I'll be right back to help you mount your horses, miss," Leo calls over his shoulder. "Your father's expecting Sarah Jac."

Neither of the girls responds. Farrah, though, won't take her eyes off me. She's judging me. Like the man who stood at the gate of the ranch the day I arrived here, Farrah's sizing me up, trying to determine my use, my worth. I'm like a mule to her, or a goat.

I want to tell her: *I stole your horse last night. Last night, it was mine.*

The littler girl keeps trying to smooth out her hair as it gets blown around by the wind. Her attempts to mimic the effortless poise of her sister are failing.

"Come on," Leo says to me. His wide grin is still there but has twisted. "Gonzales wants to talk to you."

"Where's James?" I ask, still not moving. "Is he here?"

"No. Why would he be?" His eyes scan my face. "What's wrong with you? Come on."

I follow.

There are fountains in the courtyard. They are filled with *water*, clear water that seems to serve no purpose other than to provide decoration and create a soothing sound. There are also women and men, who, unlike the jimadors in the fields, have on clothes that aren't stained with grease or nearly falling apart from wear. They're busy: raking the rocks in the courtyard into swirling patterns, carrying wicker baskets of laundry and towels, carrying large trunks. They don't look at or speak to one another. Even though they're older than me—maybe in their twenties or thirties—they remind me of the kids who work in the mess crew, absorbed in and dedicated to their work for reasons I've never quite understood. I have no idea how they resist throwing themselves into the fountains and letting that water soak into their clothes and their skin.

Leo leads me into the main house. Most of the doors and windows have been thrown open, resulting in soothing cross breezes. A large entry room is filled with furniture that is sparse and functional. There are two tanned red cowhide chairs in front of a fireplace, and a mahogany sideboard topped with a cut-glass bottle of clear liquor and a matching set of tumblers. Tall plants in terra-cotta pots have been placed in corners. Their vivid green leaves shoot upward, seven or eight feet high. It's rare to see a green so fresh and bright.

Hallways extend from this room in various dark directions. Hallways inevitably lead to bedrooms. Bedrooms can contain jewelry boxes or bureaus with drawers that have false bottoms. False bottoms are always full of the best little treasures.

I shouldn't be thinking about the treasures found in drawers, but that little Gonzales girl I saw outside has me regressing, flying back in time, waxing nostalgic. Lane and I would steal a watch. We'd sell it. Instead of using the money to buy new pairs of boots, we'd go out to a matinee and splurge on hard candy.

Thinking about boots makes me glance down to mine. I worry that they'll leave scuff marks across the owner's beautiful orange tile floor. Then I wonder why I'm worrying about that, why I'd want to stomp all over that little Gonzales girl out there but keep the floors in here spotless.

"Hey, Sarah Jac." Leo has stopped in front of a polished wood door. "Seriously. What's wrong with you?"

"Have you sold us out?" I whisper.

Leo laughs and knocks on the door. There's the sound of a squeaking chair, followed by footsteps approaching from the other side. Boot heels click-clack against tile, but there's something off in the rhythm of the steps. I take a breath and hold it as the door opens.

Gonzales is handsome in the same way his daughters are beautiful. It's a handsome that comes from eating green vegetables and living indoors. It comes from the acceptance of false compliments and forced smiles of women and workers. It's a smooth kind of handsome with no grit, so smooth it's practically a blur. Gonzales is wearing a light blue button-up shirt and pants that are made of cream-colored linen that matches the shade of the plaster that covers the walls of his house. His cologne smells like piñon pine. He's shorter than I am. His smile is halfhearted, which I imagine is how all of his smiles are.

I think to myself: this is not a man capable of creating and placing a hex on his ranch, but I've been wrong before. If he offers me something to eat or drink, I will not accept it.

Leo introduces me by name. "The girl you came across in the field yesterday," he adds. "The one who's good with horses."

I laugh. It comes out in a short hysterical burst. The sound of it ricochets through the room and out the window. I cover my mouth and glance at Leo, who's obviously confused. Gonzales' half smile, however, doesn't waver. He ushers me into the room, thanks Leo, and then promptly shuts him out.

Gonzales walks past me in the direction of his paper-littered desk. It's then that I see the limp. His left leg is the bad one. It drags. That explains the uneven sound I heard from the other side of the door. I wonder if his leg has always been that way—since birth—or if he had an accident.

He pulls out a chair upholstered in burgundy leather and tells me to sit. I reach up, debating whether or not I should remove my sun hat. My hand hovers for a moment, and I turn to face the open window behind his desk. In the fields, under a brutal sun, workers cut maguey while the foremen patrol on horseback. This is Gonzales' view every day. I lower my hand. The hat stays on.

I take my seat and wait to be spoken to.

Gonzales lowers himself into a chair behind his desk. He says I seem to know my way around a horse. "Is this true?"

"I grew up with them." Realizing I'm cracking my knuckles, I shove my hands under my thighs. "My grandmother had horses. I can break them, care for them." *Cause them to tip over and crush their riders.*

Gonzales sits back, folds his hands in his lap, and considers me for a long moment. "The reason I brought you up to the house this morning is because I need a trainer for Bell."

"I'm sorry?"

"My daughter Bell," Gonzales says. "She needs a riding

companion and someone to teach her the basics of how to handle a horse. Ideally, that person would be her sister, but Farrah isn't well and can't be out for a lengthy amount of time. I want to pair her with a young woman, as opposed to Leo or another one of the male field hands."

"No." I stand so quickly I nearly lose my balance.

Gonzales flicks his gaze down to a piece of paper on his desk, and the side of his mouth twitches. My response is obviously not what he was expecting. The truth is I would give almost anything to be with those horses, but this man can't even begin to understand how repulsive I find the idea of working with that little girl to be. Every time I'd see her, she'd remind me of Lane, and I don't want to be reminded of Lane. I want to think of my sister on *my* terms, when *I* want, recalling the memories I've shaped and collected, like lying side by side in the grass on my grandmother's farm making up stories about the clouds and the stars and sitting side by side on the roof of our building making up stories about two sisters who traveled the world. Lane, who was always encouraging me to look up and around. I can't think of her all the time, or I'll crack.

I apologize to Gonzales in my most polite tone. "You're mistaken," I add. "I know horses, but I've never given anyone lessons on how to ride before. I wouldn't even know where to start."

I crack my knuckles again and am flooded with a sense of relief. I stood my ground and am proud of it.

But then, Gonzales, still looking down, deflates me by saying

my name in a way that makes me feel as small and imperma-
nent as a graphite tick in a ledger book. "I know this meeting
is sudden for you." He lifts his gaze. "But I'm afraid you've
misunderstood the nature of it. I'm not asking you if you'd like
this job. I'm telling you that you will take it. Two days out of
the week, you will work with my daughter here in the yard and
help with the horses in their stables. The other days you'll work
in the fields cutting maguey like you normally would. Your pay
will stay the same, forty cents a day."

A moment passes. I wish I could grow wings and fly through
the window and back out to the fields.

Nothing good ever comes after the words "Let me show you
something," which is exactly what Gonzales says next. I am suddenly very tired as I watch him get up from his chair and make
his way across the room. If his leg pains him, he doesn't let on.
He stops in front of a tall glass display case full of dozens of blue
and green stones, all polished and shaped into oblong spheres
and ranging in size from a small plum to a fist. Each is displayed
on its own individual stand. Gonzales beckons for me to come
join him. I do. I don't really have a choice.

"I don't just collect them," he tells me as I approach. "I wait
for them. I travel to where they make their nests, and I wait,
sometimes for several hours. Then, when they fly away in search
of food, I climb up to their nests. If you come closer, you'll see
the holes in the sides. They have to be drained before I can display them, of course. Some of the holes are quite large because
the chicks were close to hatching when I retrieved them."

I realize then what I'm looking at and fight back a gag. Those stones aren't stones. They're eggs, egg*shells*. And yes, at least one of them has a hole in the side of it the size of a penny.

"These eggs come from species that are extraordinarily rare." Gonzales taps the glass with his clean, rounded fingernail. "Many are endangered. But, you see, I have no interest in the birds themselves. If one of these species were to become extinct, this egg would be all that's left. It would be the rarest of the rare."

I'm no longer studying the eggs but my reflection in the glass. It's been forever since I've seen myself, and my first thought is that I resemble a scarecrow stuffed with straw. My eyes are dull; there are dark rings underneath them. My dirty dark hair sticks out from beneath my hat, and the buttons on my shirt aren't properly matched with their buttonholes.

Gonzales says my name again. I meet his gaze, but since he's a few inches shorter than me, I have to tilt my chin down. This man is physically inferior to me, but he might as well be a giant. Like all jefes, Gonzales always gets what he wants, and I'm a girl who rarely gets what she wants. He knows this; he knows he has me trapped, and that makes me furious. He asks me if I know why he's telling me about his eggs, and I get the sense that this is a question he's repeated.

I want to leave this house.

"I'm devoted to the care and preservation of the rarest of the rare," he says after it's obvious that I'm not going to answer. "On a very small scale, that applies to my collection here. It more so applies to my family. I do whatever needs to be done to care and provide for my daughters."

I wait for him to tell me that the preference of some half-breed field hand means less than dirt to him because at least he can grow valuable things in dirt, but he doesn't do that. I wish he would because then I'd know what to do. I'd keep that insult. I'd fold it up. I'd tuck it deep inside, in a safe place with all of the others. That's *my* collection. That's what *I* hold dear: all the insults and all the names I've been called by people who hold positions of power—a collection so thick it could stop a bullet.

Instead he says, "You'll receive word when it's time for you to start, most likely in the next few days. The truck is waiting to take you back to the fields. I know based on how much we pay you how eager you must be to get back to work."

I'M CLIMBING INTO the bed of the idling truck, going through all the things I should've said to Gonzales, when I hear someone calling out for us to wait. It's Farrah. She runs up just before the truck takes off and smacks the side of it to get the driver's attention. Then she turns her head away to cough. It's a strange high, grating sound, almost like a whine made by a hungry dog.

"You're going to be working with my sister," she says breathlessly.

Farrah coughs again. After a moment, she straightens and adjusts her hat so I get a full view of her face. For the first time, I notice the yellow tint to the whites of her eyes and slightly grayish pallor of her skin. I see it now: the owner's rare bird is sick.

"Tell me about your cousin," she demands. "Leo said his name is James."

"What do you want to know?"

"What can he do?" Farrah asks. "Aside from harvest maguey. Leo said you two used to live in Chicago, so I'm assuming he has skills aside from harvest work. We need more hands around the house, and we were thinking he might be a good fit."

James' list of skills and former jobs runs fairly long, but I don't trust Farrah. I don't want to give away too much. "He's been a mechanic. He's worked in rail yards and steel mills. Construction and demolition."

"Farrah!" The younger one, Bell, is standing at the entrance to the house. "Papá wants you."

"Can he also ride?" Farrah asks, ignoring her sister.

"Yes."

He can ride because I taught him how. Before we came south to the maguey fields, I took him down to my grand-mother's farm. None of our animals were still there, but a black mare from somewhere else had made that land her own. She was only slightly feral, and James won her over easily, as he does.

"Does he ride *well*?" Farrah urges.

Again, her illness-dulled face reveals a disarming amount of shrewdness. She keeps her eye on things, which means I should keep my eye on her.

"Farrah!" Bell calls out.

"I heard you, Bell!" Farrah shouts over her shoulder before turning back to me. "You'll have your hands full with my sister," she says. "She gets nervous around horses. There was an accident a couple of years ago."

"Was she hurt?" I ask.

"No." Farrah hits the side of the truck as a signal to the driver to pull away. She's done with me. "At least not the way you might think."

SIX

"SHE'S DYING," LEO says. "Wasting disease. Farrah knows it. Everyone in the house knows it. The only one who refuses to accept it is Gonzales."

It's late. Hours after dinner. A group of us are sitting around a dying fire passing around a near-empty jug of pulque. I'm avoiding James, but that doesn't mean I'm not aware of him, just a few feet away, sitting thigh-to-thigh with Odette. She has to be enchanted by the saturated color of his eyes lit by firelight and flattered he's chosen to focus them on her in this moment. He says something I can't hear—something effortlessly charming, I'm sure. He smiles and reaches for her hand. She lets him interlace his fingers with hers but then leans slightly back as if she's suddenly bashful.

James pulls her toward him. Odette falls easily into his arms and rests her hand on his chest. She's so small compared to him, elegant almost, nearly weightless.

That smell she smells on him, that spice like a wild animal: that's *my* smell.

James glances my way. His eyes narrow as if to remind me that I'm the one in control, that I can say the word and we can stop this whole charade. Instead, I stare back into embers of the fire and think of him and me, tangled in our quilts, tangled in each other, out East, in our little house built into the hill.

The jug of pulque makes its way to me. Normally, I'm not much of a drinker, but the servings at dinner tonight were smaller than normal—something about beetles getting into the sacks of cornmeal—and the alcohol makes me forget I'm hungry. I take a long pull from the jug, welcome the harsh burn, and pass it to Bruno, who passes it along to Leo.

"How's the younger one dealing with it?" Bruno asks. "Her sister being sick and all?"

"She's throwing fits," Leo replies, wincing from the alcohol. "From what I gather, she's always been a pain in the ass, but now she's worse. You'll be earning your money, Sarah Jac."

I snicker.

I didn't tell James that Farrah asked about him. The possibility of James and me working at the house together seems too good to be true, and saying something might jinx it. I did tell him about the eggs—how Gonzales proudly gazed at them the way some men gaze at pictures of their handsome families, how he was trying to teach me some lesson about capturing and cherishing precious, rare things. James listened, all the while frowning down at his boots. He said it was terrible. Those baby birds still in their shells were so helpless. Life's so rare in this world that it's a shame when someone goes out and steals what's left of it.

Leo takes another pull, tipping his head back so far as to expose the entire length of his throat. He then squints to peer into the dark mouth and gives the jug a shake.

"Sorry," he says, "I guess that's the last of it."

At least now I have an excuse to leave. I rise to stand, restless to get away, for tomorrow to come so I can get back into the rhythm of my work and have some control over myself.

"I can walk you back to your bunkhouse, Sarah Jac," Bruno offers, also standing. He's taller than me by at least half a foot, wide and solidly built. He seems like the gentle giant type, like he'd be warm to the touch or like he'd be able to shield me from cold night winds. The first couple of buttons on his shirt are undone, revealing the edges of his collarbones. There's a tattoo there, something written in cursive, spanning the length of his upper chest. I want to know what those words are, what they mean, what kinds of secrets they hold.

My eyes track up Bruno's face, and he grins. He knows where my attention has been. His smile is generous, genuine, unlike tricky Leo's. I've never kissed a guy as big as Bruno before. I wonder what it would feel like to be wrapped up by his arms, thickly corded with muscle, and enveloped in the sweet scent of the tobacco he uses in his cigarettes. I would kiss the ink on his skin. He holds out his massive hand, and I should take it.

Instead, I shake my head. "I'll manage by myself, thanks."

Averting my eyes from James and Odette, I make my way through the now-familiar darkness to the bunkhouse. Once there, I fall onto the thin, bare mattress.

I breathe in through my nose and release a loud, rattling exhale. Some people say it takes time to adjust to a new bed, but those people don't know what my life has been like. Some nights in Chicago, I slept on benches or in stairways, with Lane huddled up close, the both of us shivering. Any bed is better than none. I lay there trying to push out thoughts of James and Odette and replace them with thoughts about sun and work and songs in four-four time. I try to imagine Bruno beside me, warming me up in various ways.

But instead, I think about That Time Outside Tulsa.

That's what I call it, anyway. James doesn't talk about it at all.

We were just off the train from Chicago, the first train we ever jumped. We had stars in our eyes. We were bulletproof. We were stupid.

We had no idea about betrayal and its motivations—how a person could sell out someone else for a glass of cold water or a sandwich, how it was best to assume that no one ever did anything "out of the kindness of his heart," and how all favors had to be repaid in one way or another.

That Time Outside Tulsa was the reason we started to pretend we're cousins. There was a jimador, a guy our age who was itching to work his way up to foreman. He and I cut maguey in the same fields while James worked as a mechanic, fixing trucks back at camp. During water breaks this guy would sit next to me, give me extra pieces of his jerky, offer up pointers on how to better use a coa and cut more maguey in less time. He taught me a lot. He said he'd been working in the fields for about a year, jumping trains by himself, following the harvests. He told me he thought James and I had something really special because we came out here together and that to see someone committed to another person was really rare these days. Having protection out here in the desert was a hard thing to come by, he said. He also wanted to give me a word of warning—to not make it so obvious that James and I were together. Not to hang all over each other around the campfire and whatnot.

Just last season it happened, he said. Here, outside Tulsa. There was a couple, a girl who wove strips of faded cloth in her hair to look like ribbons and the boy who loved her. They were inseparable. They worked side by side in the field, ate off the same plate at mealtimes. Sometimes, at the campfire, she took the fabric out of her hair and wove it into his.

One morning, both of them showed up in the coa line, and it was obvious something very bad had happened. Her eye sockets were purple and black from where they'd broken her nose. He had a bandage around a deep vertical cut they'd made in the soft skin of his elbow crease. A cut like that would take forever to heal and make it nearly impossible to work.

"Do you understand what I'm trying to tell you?" the guy asked me.

I took a guess: "People were jealous?"

"That." The guy shrugged. "And money. They made threats. Told the boy to hand over his wages or they'd do worse to his girl. It's the easiest and oldest con in the book."

"What happened to them?" I asked.

"They left." He paused. "Or they tried to leave. One of the foremen found what was left of them out in the plain. The circling turkey vultures led them to their bodies." He placed his hand on my knee. "I just don't want you to end up like her, Sarah Jac."

I remember nodding my head like I understood, even though I didn't. I wasn't as good then at reading signs as I am now. I didn't notice the way he'd sit so close to me that our knees would touch, or how his fingers would linger too long on my hand when he was showing me how to use my coa, or how I'd catch him staring at me across the campfire after he'd been drinking pulque, or how he'd tell me I'd look better if I cut my hair, or how—toward the end—he'd sometimes call me by some other girl's name. Rita. Or Diana. Something like that.

I did notice, however, when, on the night of a bonfire, I was standing next to James and laughing, and the guy suddenly charged up, pulled me to him, and violently slammed his pulque-soaked lips into mine. I threw the first punch; James threw the second. The guy swung back hard enough to break James' nose before the fight was finally broken up and everyone staggered back to their bunkhouses.

The next morning we found out one of the foremen had

been killed. He'd been keeping watch when someone snuck up on him from behind and stabbed him through the ribs with his own knife. He'd been robbed of his watch, stripped of all the cheap brass buttons on his coat, and left to the coyotes that had torn off chunks of his face in the night.

We were all brought out into the yard while the overseer searched our bunks. Eventually, he came out holding a knife and a watch. He claimed he found the items under one of the mattresses.

"James Holt," he called out.

They led James away. There was a man on either side of him gripping his arms, and one behind, holding a rifle to his back to keep him moving. James swiveled his head to try and find me in the crowd, but the foreman behind him mashed the double barrels of his gun against his cheek.

I had to work that day, but I don't remember much about it. I do remember that when we got back to camp in the afternoon, I went around to the back of the bathhouse and threw up in a ditch until I was dizzy.

Later that night was the first time I woke to James' hand clamped down over my mouth. He was not smiling then, like he was when he brought me to see Britain. That night, That Time Outside Tulsa, his eyes were filled with a frightening, near-blank expression I hadn't seen before and haven't seen since. His hand was slick with sweat.

We spent the rest of that night running through the frigid wilderness and then the following day delirious and half dead of thirst as the turkey vultures swooped overhead. I swore that if we lived we'd be smart enough to not end up like the boy and the girl with the ribbons.

Finally, somehow, we caught a train south. By then, of course, I'd realized that James' hand hadn't been slick with sweat, but with blood.

SEVEN

TWO MORNINGS AFTER my first trip to the Gonzales house, I'm called back to work with Bell and the horses. I watch Leo approach from the direction of the house while I'm standing at the end of the coa line, waiting to get what I'm sure will be another dull tool.

"Ready?" he asks.

"As I'll ever be."

At the stables, Leo offers me some fresh-boiled coffee, which I refuse. This was one of my grandmother's rules: don't drink coffee and never eat breakfast. She believed it weakened a person's spirit and hindered her ability to make clear decisions.

In the yard, both Farrah's Britain and her father's white horse are already saddled. Bell is there, too, dressed in a tidy pair of overalls. Her cowboy boots are stiff from lack of use and shine like a polished red apple. Her orange-gold hair is tied back in a braid. It glows in the early-morning sun.

She's smaller than I remember, as if her sister's illness has shaved away her own bones. I can't help hoping she eventually disappears into nothing.

Leo introduces me: "Bell, this is Sarah Jac. She's going to help you figure your way around a horse."

The girl doesn't reply. She just gazes, blankly. I've seen vacant looks like this in kids' eyes before, but usually in those of Chicago orphans, and usually after they've figured out that someone has left them and is never coming back, or that their stomachs are always going to growl, or that the blood they've been coughing up is a sign of something much worse than a common cold.

"Hey!" I wave my hand in the girl's face. She hardly blinks. "Have you ever even been on a horse?"

Leo leans in. "She has, but there was an accident."

"You were bucked?" I ask. "Your sister mentioned something."

"Charged, I think."

I point to the white stallion. "By this one?"

"A different one," Leo replies. "They got rid of it."

I walk toward the stallion, clicking my tongue and trying to get its attention. As I pass Bell, she mumbles something I can't hear. I stop.

"Did you say something?"

"Don't talk about me like I'm not here," the little girl says quietly.

"Then you should learn to answer questions." I grab the

girl's chin and force her eyes up to meet mine. "And to look at people when they're talking to you."

Bell's expression isn't exactly blank, I now realize. It's simmering. Anger radiates from her pale, cactus-green eyes. I understand anger, and I understand *her* anger—her sister is very sick, after all. That's got to saw at a young girl's nerves. But Bell is spoiled. Her entire life, she's been protected and valued and assured a future full of hot food and soft beds. She has *expectations*. James and I have always had our plans, but plans are different from expectations. Expectations are firm. You expect the stars to appear at night because they've always appeared at night. If they didn't, you'd think the world was ending. Plans are more like half dreams. They can change; the best ones are flexible. If a plan is derailed, your heart may crack, but it won't fully break because you can always modify the plan and create a different route to the end.

These are complicated distinctions I would never expect a little girl to understand.

I release Bell and continue over to the white horse. His nostrils flare as I approach, and he kicks the ground. When I touch his neck, the skin ripples under my hand. He's sending out warning signs, but I know his type. He's powerful and in search of an opponent.

But I don't feel like being this horse's opponent today. I leave him and head to Britain. She's much different from the stallion; her energy smolders below a calm surface. I stroke her long face. Her breath is warm and even.

"You don't have anything to prove, do you?" I coo.

My gaze shifts back to Bell. She's staring at the ground, drawing circles in the dust with the toe of her boot.

"We'll ride together," I call out. "You can sit on the saddle in front of me." Bell doesn't respond, just keeps making her circles. "No running. Just walking. Maybe a trot. We don't even have to talk to each other if that's what you want."

Those were the magic words.

WE HEAD OUT together, me and this sack of bones called Bell. Even though Britain is young, I trust her sense of direction and let her take us anywhere she wants to go. Whenever the horse approaches a trot, Bell tenses up, so I keep us reined in to a mid-tempo walk.

Our ride, as I promised, is silent, but after an hour or so, my head starts to throb. The direct sun and my growing thirst have started taking their toll, so I steer the horse around to what I'm fairly certain is the direction of home. We've seen no animals—not even a lizard—but eventually, a group of three black birds soars soundlessly through the sky, from right to left, north to south.

When the ranch house is visible in the near distance, Bell speaks for the first time.

"I like birds," she says.

This is actually a sort of perfect thing for her to say.

"So do I."

• • •

THAT NIGHT, LEO gets in another fight, and this time, I'm around to witness it. It happens at the campfire, after dinner. Some words are exchanged. I don't know what they are, and it doesn't really matter. All I see is Leo reach into the fire, snatch up the end of a thick mesquite branch, and hurl it toward some guy I've seen around but have never spoken to. The guy shields his face as the glowing hunk of wood explodes against his arms. He releases a feral growl and then leaps across the fire to tackle Leo. Together they slam into the dirt and become a tangle of limbs and fists. James rushes over from where he's sitting with Odette, clamps on to Leo, and pulls him away. Once free, the other guy stumbles to his feet, pauses, and then launches his fist into James' face. I wince, and so does half of camp. It's a good, square hit. James' head twists up and back, and Leo falls from his arms. Odette lets out a squeak, and then, for the shortest of moments, the camp goes quiet. I take a breath in and hold it.

Leo's sprawled on the ground, and James neatly steps over his long legs. His hands are clenched into fists. The other guy stands alone, back to the fire, taking heaving breaths. His forearms are white, covered in ash and newly forming blisters.

"Why would you defend him?" the guy shouts to James, spitting into the dirt. "He'll pretend to be your friend, but it's all an act!"

If James knows what the guy is talking about, he doesn't let on. James has been challenged. His friend, Leo, has been challenged. He has to prove his strength and his loyalty. For so many of us, these are the only things we have.

James huffs out a breath, draws a line in the dirt with the toe of his boot, and steps back. The other guy comes forward, shuffling on unsteady feet, and makes a clumsy attempt at a right hook with an arm obviously in pain. This time, James dodges away easily and then lands a punch of his own. It connects with the guy's left eye socket. He goes down hard, his legs crumpling underneath him. He's out cold before his head even hits the ground.

I'm about to run over to James, but Odette beats me to it. She flies into his arms, planting kisses all over his face, examining him for cuts and bruises, overdoing it as usual. Leo stands, dusts off his clothes, and claps James on the back. The other guy's buddies hover around him, slap him in the face, pour water on him until he's shocked awake.

Odette's kisses have found their way to James' mouth, and she is stuck there. She crushes him with her worry and reaches up to twine her fingers tightly into his hair. James has his hand on the small of Odette's back. His fingers are splayed; their tips press into the worn fabric of her cotton dress.

I never have gotten used to the sudden, piercing pain in my chest that comes along with a scene like this. I can feel my eyes pool up. I can't help it, and I'm pissed that I can't help it.

Just know the whole thing will be over the second you say it's over, James told me no more than a week ago.

The desert, Leo said before that, *it seems so simple and boring, but really it's full of secrets.*

I turn away from the campfire and march back to the bunkhouse.

Hard hearts.

PART TWO

THE PROPHET

EIGHT

ON MY FIRST night at the Real Marvelous, we were served spit-fired beef, collards, and cornbread sweetened with agave nectar. In the fields, the foremen would give us jerky and dried fruit—figs, sometimes even apricots—during our breaks. Now, over two weeks later, we eat mostly beans, flavored with what tastes like rancid salt pork, and there are no more snacks out in the field.

The cornmeal is officially ruined. Almost every burlap sack the mess crew opens has something in it that's not supposed to be there: ants, beetles, centipedes, cicada husks, moths. There's a rumor that one of the sacks was filled with sand instead of meal, and out of the sand crawled a lizard the size of a brick. When the lizard opened its mouth, a bee flew out. That bee stung one of the mess kids on the hand, which then swelled up so bad, it had to be lanced. The kid nearly died. Now no one can get him to talk anymore. He won't even say his name. We wonder if he even remembers it.

We can live off pork-flavored beans if we need to, but that's not the point. Not having enough food—or even the threat of not having enough food—makes people get weird. They hoard—not just food, but bits of soap from the bathhouse, buttons they find in the dirt, and strands of other people's hair. Rosa, who bunks above me, keeps a mouse in her pillowcase. She feeds it scraps from dinner, and I'm forced to hear it munching and squeaking all night.

Almost every evening at supper, the overseer, in his mirrored sunglasses and with his mastiffs at his side, attempts to soothe us. He says the ranch is doing the best it can. The wells are still producing water. There are scouts out trying to find reliable sources for grain. These are drought conditions, he tells us, as if we didn't already know that. Aside from maguey, nothing is really growing. The small number of livestock is getting thin and sick. The earth won't change.

While that explanation is *sound*, that doesn't make it *good*. Fuses are getting short. Tempers are flaring. Fights are breaking out in the fields and in the coa lines.

One morning, Bruno got knocked in the head with a rifle butt for working too slow and then had his pay docked for telling off the foreman who hit him. Parents are starting to teach their kids how to con the mess crew into second helpings of food. There's more sex. I can hear it at night in the bunkhouses and in the shadows behind the buildings: moans, slaps, shouts, laughter.

And then there are the accidents. Cutting maguey takes a certain amount of skill and focus, and if you're tired or weak or green, you can make a mistake. A mistake with a coa can have gruesome consequences. Every few days, a scream rises from somewhere in the field. The red-black color of fresh blood stands out against the dust, and I'm always surprised how fast blood can gush out of a wound to the shoulder or the shin—and I'm also surprised how quickly the ground can soak that blood up.

WE'RE ON A water break, the second in an hour. The day has been particularly hot—the kind of hot that pulses on the horizon. A couple of workers have already gone crazy from it. They started blabbing and stripping off their clothes and then stumbled off in the direction of that pulsing horizon. The other workers had to round them up, calm them down, coax water down their throats, and usher them to the trucks so they could be driven back to camp. I'm trying to ignore the creeping tendrils of a headache that always seem to be wrapping around my skull.

"It's not fair you get to work at the house," Odette says before gulping down water from her tin cup.

"I've only been there a few times. And it's not like I'm actually *in* the house. Honestly, I'd rather be cutting maguey."

Odette starts talking about James. I've been doing a good job of ignoring the two of them at mealtimes, but Odette still finds ways to seek me out in the bunkhouse or the bathhouse and pry: *Has he said anything about me lately? He told me last night he had a girlfriend back in Chicago. Why did they break up? Did she look anything like me?*

I tune her out by focusing on the horizon. There's something out there, a bobbing and shimmering shape in the distance, coming our way. It may be a coyote or a horse, but as I watch it, I realize it's a person: a woman—or maybe a girl. She doesn't come from the direction of the train tracks, but from the direction of the mountains. She's alone.

Despite the oppressive heat, she's wearing what appears to be a fur cap on her head.

Before she can reach us, one of the foremen goes out, intercepts her, guides her into a truck, and takes her back to camp. Another foreman blows his whistle and tells us to get back to work.

When I get back to camp that afternoon, I notice that the stranger who walked straight out of the mountains has chosen a bunk near mine. She's asleep on her back, with her mouth closed and her arms across her chest like a corpse posed in a casket. Her fur cap hangs on the edge of her cot, and her head's shorn of all hair. She's still asleep when I come back from supper. She gets up, finally, just as the rest of us are settling in for the night. She sits on the edge of her bunk, staring at me as I yawn and remove my boots. When I notice her, I stop and stare back.

"I'm Eva," she says.

"Hi, Eva," I reply.

"You're full of hate," she declares, so simply, so without guile, as if it's just some ordinary observation.

"Oh, yeah?" I grin. "Well, you're full of shit."

THE NEXT MORNING, Eva steps up onto an overturned crate and announces to us all that she has "gifts" to share. She sees things, she tells us, things that other people don't have the ability to see. She can help us. Her timing could not be better. Eva has arrived at the exact moment when camp is tilting toward ruin and the jimadors are searching for someone to set their world right again.

Three nights later, a group of girls crowd around Eva's bunk, where she's lying, faceup, spouting her prophecies. She's been speaking nonstop of magic and doom, and the jimadors, if they love anything, it's a story about magic and doom.

She says, "There will be a plague."

I roll over on my cot and pull the thin blanket over my head.

The girls beg to know: *What kind of plague?*

I wonder why that even matters. A plague's a plague. All kinds are, by definition, terrible.

"A plague of pests, small pests," she tells them.

Rats, Eva? They sound so worried. *Or locusts?*

Eva says, "The details are unclear."

They ask: *When will the plague come?*

"Soon," Eva says. "There is a witch in our midst. She's the one who will bring the plague. She's the one who has cursed the ground. She's causing the crops to die. Soon, there will be no water. Soon, the winds will rise up, and there will be a storm that lasts for weeks. After that, the ranch will be no more. It will be covered by dunes. This storm will break our hearts and our bodies. To prepare, you must get clean. Only those who are pure of heart will be spared."

The girls mutter among themselves. I hear them shuffle, searching for something. I open an eye and see one of them holding a pair of rusty scissors she must have stolen from the supply shed.

The next morning, the fields are full of girls who've cut off their hair. All that's left are ragged clumps and nicks in scalps.

That same day, in the high afternoon, while Odette and I are in the maguey fields working just down the row from each other, I hear a horrific scream. Odette's coa falls to the ground next to where her boot is coated in blood. A chunk of flesh sits in a cut piece of leather in the dust—a toe. Odette stumbles to the side, goes pale, and then throws up. I manage to rush over and catch her just before she passes out.

Later, in the bunkhouse, Eva celebrates Odette for her injury. She tells her that only through pain can a person get pure.

I don't know if Odette feels pure, but she certainly feels pain. Her wound bled for a long time, the blood pulsing in time with her heartbeat and soaking into the dirt until a truck came to take her back to camp. Her toe was left behind. I eventually kicked a pile of dirt on top of it because that seemed like the decent thing to do rather than just leave it there for the ants.

Odette's foot has been stitched and is wrapped in cloth bandages, but she's still pale and trembling. Her long blond hair is damp and stuck to her cheeks. Her eyes are unfocused, her gaze zigzagging. She might not even be hearing a word of Eva's praise.

But Rosa listens, from the bunk above mine. I can hear her up there, the sound of her fingers tapping the bundle of sticks that hangs around her neck. The twigs crunch and pop. Her little mouse squeaks.

"You should welcome the pain, Odette," Eva says. "You should continue to find the root of your evil and cut it out."

NINE

BELL WATCHES A black bird circle overhead. She says, "There's something wrong with my sister."

The little girl is sitting in front of me on the saddle. The sweat from the back of her shirt transfers to the front of mine. Even after a handful of rides, if the horse comes close to a trot, Bell stiffens. So, we walk. I feel bad for Britain. This must be torture for her.

"She'll get better," I offer.

"Do you have a sister?" Bell asks.

"Yes." I shift in my saddle. "She's . . . somewhere else."

"Do you miss her?"

"Sometimes."

"Where are your parents?"

In all our days of so-called riding lessons, maybe four in all, this is the most I've ever heard Bell talk. I try to compare her voice to Lane's, but I've forgotten what Lane's voice sounded like.

"I don't have parents," I say. "I grew up in a home for girls. Lots of girls from cities grew up in places like that."

This is only sort of true. My grandmother raised me until I was thirteen. I buried her myself, under an oak tree at the edge of her property. She told me where she wanted her body to go and taught me how to dig a grave so I'd know how when the time came. After that, Lane and I lived by ourselves on our grandmother's farm until one of our neighbors called the authorities. Then we were dragged off to Chicago. I barely had time to send the horse off and let the animals out to pasture.

"My mother was bucked from a horse," Bell says. "Papá says it was my fault because I got mad right before she went out to ride." Then, like flipping a switch: "I think we should go back now. The shadows." She points to the ground. She's right. We've been gone longer than I'd planned, and the shadows made by our bodies have stretched long and thin.

"Papá loves Farrah, but he doesn't love me."

"I'm sure that's not true," I say, thinking of Gonzales and his eggs, and about the lengths he'll go to preserve the rarest of the rare. "Some people show their love in strange ways."

I make a clicking sound and pull Britain into a turn, but we've only gone about half a mile when the horse jolts backward and then trips. Bell shrieks and pitches sideways in the saddle. I work to steady the horse while scanning the ground for a snake. Britain snorts, shakes her head frantically, and, as Bell cries out again, takes off into an uneven canter.

I grip Bell around her waist and take the reins in one hand. The little girl twists and squeals. How can she be so slippery?

"Calm down!" I shout. "It was just a snake!"

"It wasn't a snake!" Bell clutches my arm. "It was bees! One of them landed on my leg!"

I manage to pull Britain to a stop, but she's obviously agitated. I guide her around in a quick circle so that I can search the sky for a mass of hovering specks. I listen for a hum. There's nothing. Just wind and desert.

"It's fine," I say. "Britain might've gotten stung, but she's fine. You want me to run her back to the ranch?"

"No!" Bell shakes her head so furiously her hat almost flies off.

Bell's survival instincts are terrible. She wants saving from imaginary bees and then she doesn't. I slide my arm out from around her so I can take the reins in each of my hands and then coax an uneasy Britain into a walk.

If what Bell said is true, if her dad doesn't love her, then of course I feel sorry for her. Lane and I didn't know our dads, so we couldn't know what it was like to be blamed for something in such a cruel way. It's tough to tell how Farrah is with her sister. Aside from that first day, I haven't seen them together. Lane and I were inseparable, each other's shadows.

She was eleven when she died. It happened in Chicago, at the tail end of winter, when it had been sleeting for days on end. That morning James said he was going to take Lane out to get a new coat—hers had been threadbare and in tatters for months—but he'd lied. He'd taken her to a carnival. He won her a cheap stuffed bear by knocking over a tower of milk bottles with a baseball. They rode that god-awful Ferris wheel that rocked and wailed even when the weather was decent. They drank hot cocoa and ate kettle corn, all paid for with money James had won in cards the night before.

Lane was already feverish by the time the two of them got back to our room. I stripped off Lane's wet clothes and wrapped her in a wool blanket, but within hours her temperature spiked. We didn't take her to the hospital because hospitals cost money and James had gone and spent too much at the carnival. Instead, we threw open all the windows to keep Lane cool and took turns running to the tap at the end of the hall to wet a cloth to lay across her forehead.

"It's my fault," James said, as if that needed saying. Lane was sleeping, breathing noisily out of her mouth. "I'll fix it. Tomorrow. I'll find a game."

I held my tongue because I didn't want Lane to wake up and hear me yelling at James, but I wanted more than anything to heap layer upon layer of blame on him until he was crushed by the weight of it. It *was* his fault. He shouldn't have taken her out, no matter how many times she asked. She was *my* sister. How could he be so careless with her?

James left the next morning before the sun had risen and when Lane's fever appeared to be breaking. But then she died within the hour, and things went to shit.

When James finally came home, I tried to bring the walls down with my screams. I railed at him and demanded he look at me while I did it. *He* did this; if he'd just gone out and bought my sister a coat like he said he'd do, Lane would still be alive. I told him I wished I'd never met him, that he ruined my life and killed my sister. He *killed* my sister.

James said nothing. He didn't try to touch me. He was breaking down. I could see it—in his posture, in the way his spine seemed to curve forward as if he was being eaten from the inside out. He nodded his head, heavy on that bent spine, as if he understood, as if he deserved all the blame and would accept whatever punishment I saw fit.

I kept Lane's body with me in that room for two days. Eventually, James called the undertaker. He had to hold me back as Lane was carted off. The whole time I was screaming, and James kept taking it.

My sister would've been buried outside the city limits in a pauper's grave, but James won a burial plot for her that night in a game of cards. So there was that, at least. No grave marker. But I will give her one, eventually. It'll be small—I'll never be able to afford anything big—but it'll be something with her name on it: Lane Maria Crow.

After my sister died, I stopped going to the diner I was working at and got fired. Most days I just slept. I think James knew that if we stayed in Chicago, I'd die in that room like my sister. He came up with the idea of us catching trains and seeing the country. He reminded me of the stories I used to tell him about growing up with my grandmother and how I always reminisced about working with my hands out in wide-open spaces. I didn't want to go with him at first, but he eventually convinced me with this: we'd make more money cutting maguey in the big desert than we'd know what to do with, and the first thing we'd do when we could afford it was come back to Chicago and buy Lane a proper headstone.

That was when our plans began.

It took a while—months—but I eventually apologized for all the things I'd said when Lane died. I told him there was no one to blame—not him, not me. Lane dying was just one of the cruel realities of life. People came down with fever; some of those people died. That's just how things work.

James took my hand in his. He grazed his thumb across my roughened palm and said nothing.

James *still* blames himself for Lane's death. I know he does.

I hate that Bell makes me think about this.

TEN

EVA IS PREACHING. She's hopped onto a tree stump near the campfire. Cast in the flickering light and wearing that hat of hers, she looks like she's made of beasts and magic. She tells everyone to listen, reminds us of her visions, and then claims those visions are never wrong.

"Did you hear about the California quakes, the big ones that nearly split the state in two?" she asks.

"Yes!" someone shouts.

Of course we had all heard about that.

"I foresaw those," she claims. "I felt cracks in my bones a day before those quakes hit. I was in so much pain I could hardly move. And those hurricanes that destroyed the Texas Gulf? Remember those?" Murmurs of assent ripple through the crowd. "For three straight days before they came, I was hit with wave after wave of nausea. It was at least a week after the storm passed before I could find enough balance to walk on my own two feet."

I glance over to where James is sitting with Odette. He's looking down into his bowl of runny beans, smirking. Odette, however, has gone absolutely still.

Eva lifts her hands to the sky and repeats her warning about a plague of small pests. "They are coming!" she proclaims, scratching violently at her arm. "Even now I feel them crawling across my skin. You are being punished for your evil deeds and for living wickedly, but it is not too late. I can save you!"

I can save you—these are the magic words. Several more jimadors stop eating to listen to Eva's message. They balance their plates on their knees, stop with their cups lifted midway to their lips. Even after a lifetime of this life and this work, people still hold out hope for a savior. I watch as Odette starts to fiddle with blood-crusted bandages around her foot. James has modified her boot—cut away some more of the leather, spliced the laces—so that she can hobble around the maguey fields and work again.

Eva demands again that we all get clean. "No more meat!" she shouts. "No more pulque! No more gambling."

It's too much. James grins so wide it tugs at the scar on his lip.

Alone and in the dark, I smile, too.

AFTER HELPING ODETTE back to the bunkhouse, James returns to the campfire, along with Leo, Bruno, and a jug of pulque. I can tell by the way they're walking—all off-rhythm and clumsy, like the injured Odette—that Leo and Bruno are already drunk.

"I predict . . . !" Leo exclaims, mimicking Eva by throwing his arms to the sky. "I predict, uh . . ."

Bruno removes the half-smoked cigarette from his mouth, pulls out the cork of the jug with his teeth, and spits it onto the ground. "Eva's a much better prophet than you, Leo."

James laughs, and Leo snickers.

"I'm serious." Bruno plops down next to me.

I'm warm from the fire, but Bruno's large body heats me up even more. There's a knot on his forehead and a mottled bruise above his eye from where he was hit with the rifle. I reach out and skim it with the pads of my fingers.

James turns his head to the side.

"You talked about stuff rising up from the ground," Bruno says to Leo. His voice lowers as he leans ever-so-slightly into my touch. "Eva talks about stuff coming out of the air. Her version is way scarier."

I think that's true as well. The sky seems bigger than the ground, bigger and more out of control. I've heard of earthquakes but never felt one. Storms, though—I've been in so many of those, all different kinds.

Leo ignores Bruno and stands in front of me. "Bell likes you."

I snort.

"Seriously. She says she likes you because you don't treat her like she's a baby."

"Well, she's not a baby, so . . ."

James pulls a crate across from me, flips it, and sits. My hand moves from Bruno's forehead into his dark hair, but I'm watching James out of the corner of my eye. Our knees are less than a yard apart. I can smell him, his smoke and oil smell. He scoots his foot toward mine a couple of inches, then retreats. This is code. It means: *Stop whatever you're doing with Bruno.* It means: *I want everyone to leave so that I can have you and your hands to myself.*

"You should put in a good word for James," I say to Leo. "He could work at the house with us."

James tenses, sitting up a little straighter.

"Farrah mentioned something about it," I add.

"Farrah mentioned *me*?" James asks. "When exactly did this happen?"

Before I can answer, Bruno leans in, nuzzles my cheek with his nose, and plants an unexpected, tender kiss on my temple. I lean into it; I can't help it. James scoots his boot forward again, nudging the toe of his against mine.

"It was that morning when I first went up to the house," I say. "When Gonzales told me about my new job. Farrah stopped me as I was leaving and asked what kind of work you can do." I smirk. "Maybe she . . ."

Likes you, I silently finish. But then, what started as a joke swiftly bends into something else. A plan forms: one in which the object of James' affection shifts from desperate Odette to frail Farrah. If he gains access to her, he gains access to the house, and, even better, its treasures. There might be one thing, just *one small thing*, hidden in the depths of a drawer or the recesses of a closet, that he can pocket when she's not looking.

Then we can flee to the nearest town, hock that one small thing, and be in our house in the hill.

All this time, my fingers have been against Bruno's skin, in his hair, but now I drop my hand and fold it with the other in my lap. It's started to tremble. James glances down, so quick anyone else would miss it. A puzzled, expectant expression settles onto his face. Even in the dark, he gleams. He's irresistible, even to a ranch owner's daughter who's so high above him in class she might as well be in the sky.

Leo clears his throat, and I turn my head at the sound. He cocks his eyebrow, questioning. Leo waits, but I say nothing. "I'll see what I can do," he offers. "About James. And the house."

"Leaving so soon?" James asks.

"Yes, yes," Leo replies. "Good night, cousins." He begins to stumble off in the direction of his bunkhouse, then stops. "Bruno, come with. We need to work on forming our rival cult. Let's round us up some followers."

Bruno gives my knee a squeeze and goes off with Leo. James and I wait, listening to the sound of twin sets of boots shuffling across the earth.

"What was that about?" he asks once he's sure we're alone.

"I want you close." My fingers reach up and grip the collar of his shirt and then search for skin. "If I can get you a job in the house, then I can have you near me. Besides, if you're able to worm your way into Farrah's good graces, she may let slip where her father keeps their money stashed, or their jewelry."

"Worm my way?" James lifts his hand and rests his thumb on my bottom lip.

"You know what I mean."

"I *do* know what you mean," he says, his eyes holding steady on my mouth and making my pulse race. "But I seriously doubt the ranch owner's proper daughter wants anything to do with a grubby field hand."

I swallow. "Clearly, you haven't read enough romance novels."

"Clearly." His fingers move to skim the line of my jaw, and he leans in to whisper. "But I do know that girls often fall for the big and strong type."

I huff out a laugh. "Bruno's very big and very warm. It's hard to resist."

"*I* can keep you warm."

"I know," I say, nearly breathless.

"I want to be closer to you, Sarah, so I won't turn down a job at the house. But I'm already conning one poor girl. I don't look forward to doing it to another, especially one who's dying. You wouldn't want me to be that cruel, would you?"

That word—*cruel*—it stings.

"But I've got my own idea," James says, his lips grazing across mine. "A new plan."

"Oh, yeah?"

We are co-conspirators again.

"One day, while the owner's out," he whispers, "you and I

will go into the house and steal his eggs. We'll find out where each of them came from, and we'll return them—one by one."

I laugh. What's a bird going to do with an empty shell? Aside from that, their nests are probably long gone.

My lips land on the corner of James' mouth, at his scar. I can feel him smile.

"Think of all the trees you'll get to climb," I say.

THE FOLLOWING AFTERNOON, a truck pulls up to where James is working a couple of rows over from me. After a brief exchange, James sets down his coa and hops in the back. I watch him disappear in a cloud of dust.

He doesn't come back to the field that day, and he's not in line for supper.

The next morning, Leo comes to get me to ride with Bell. Together we walk up the hill to the ranch house, and there, on a ladder, patching up the plaster on one of the exterior walls, is James.

"Meet the new groundskeeper," Leo says. "Just like you wanted."

Just like I wanted.

James climbs down the ladder just as Bell emerges from the house. She sees him and smiles, all bashful.

"Well, good morning." James goes over, places a hand on Bell's shoulder, and leans in. "You know you have the best riding instructor there is. Sarah Jac grew up around horses and has never met one she can't tame. She can also ride faster than anyone I've ever seen."

"James . . ." I don't want him talking about me to her like that. He used to do the same thing with Lane: lean in and lower his voice, like they were in on some grand secret. "She doesn't even really want to learn. Her father's forcing her."

James straightens up, shrugs. "Teach her something else, then."

"Like what?" Like lying, stealing, sprinting to catch a train?

"You know a lot about plants."

I snicker.

"Or what about the violin?"

"There's no violin here." The words are out of my mouth before I can stop them, and I have no idea if they're true or not.

Why is James doing this? He has to see that Bell reminds me of Lane, of what I lost, and what I'll never have again. I can feel my lips twist into a scowl, but he's just leaning casually against the ladder, wiping the sweat off his brow with a forearm covered in white plaster, and grinning at the sunshine.

"You can play music?" And there it is, in Bell's tone: interest, maybe even wonder. Exactly what I didn't want.

"Probably not anymore." I turn away from the house—and from James, who I don't want to even look at right now—and make my way over to the yard. "It's been a while. Let's go. The horse is waiting."

"But you could still teach me?" Bell's behind me. I can hear her running to catch up.

"Do you even have a violin?" I shout over my shoulder. "Is there one in the house?"

"No."

"Well then, no. I can't teach you." I spin around, and Bell stops short. "Besides, your dad doesn't want you to learn music. He wants you to learn how to ride."

"Violins are good luck," Bell says. "They ward off bad spirits."

"Who told you that?"

"My mom. She said that the music they make calms down angry spirits."

I don't know what to say. I've never heard anything like that, but as far as folktales go, this one isn't half bad.

ELEVEN

JAMES IS DOING this thing he does with a knife. It's a little like that trick when someone shoots an arrow through an apple that's perched on someone's head, but we don't have an arrow or an apple. It's always better when there's a crowd—in this case it's people who work in the Gonzales house, gathered together in the kitchen drinking coffee before the family wakes for breakfast—and when there's some betting involved. The trick is, I hold the end of a spoon—the thin end—between my lips. James stands off to my side and a ways away. He squints as he aims, hesitating as if he's not quite sure, as if he hasn't done this a hundred times before. He cocks his hand back quick and then releases the knife. My eyes are closed as I feel the spoon ripped from my mouth and hear it clatter to the floor.

A cheer goes up, and coins are dropped onto the table. James scoops them up and deposits them into his pockets, and I take a shuddering breath to release my built-up nerves.

"What are you going to do about that?" I ask, gesturing to the knife, stuck in the wall above the stove.

James grins. "Fix it. That's my job now."

He walks over and tugs the knife free. James blows the white dust—flecks of plaster, the eggshell color of which matches the bone of the handle—from its blade and crouches to slide his knife back into his boot.

"Nice trick."

Farrah is standing in the doorway to the kitchen, dressed in dark pants and the whitest of white shirts, as if there was any occasion out here in the desert for a stark white shirt. The early-morning sun streams in, catching on her copper curls, lighting her up, making her glow. The workers scatter out the back door, into hallways, as if she's something to fear.

"Like I said, miss, I'll fix it," James says, standing. "Right away."

Farrah walks over to the stove and lifts the percolator from the burner before its contents boil over. "You're not ever scared he's going to miss?" she asks me.

"I'd be more scared if I looked. So I never do."

Farrah pours herself a cup of coffee and then turns to lean back against the counter. She tries to make it seem casual, but I can tell by the jerky way she shifts her weight that she needs the support. Farrah's not ashamed of her weakness, though. Even as she brings the cup to her lips, she holds my gaze. Then she smiles.

"That's the better wager, then, isn't it? Not if James can hit the spoon, but if you can keep your eyes open to see it." Farrah pauses to take a sip of her coffee. The steam curls around her cheeks. "It'll probably be hot again today. You should get started with Bell."

This is an order, not a suggestion.

"I have to warn you, though, she talked back to Papá last night at dinner, so he sent her to her room without supper. She's likely to be in one of her moods."

THE MORNING IS bright and still, and there are no clouds in the sky. There's no wind, either, so when the screams start from down at camp, they're carried cleanly up to where Leo and I stand in the horse yard, waiting with Britain for a moody Bell.

We move without thinking, both of us launching over the gate and bolting down the hill. I call out once for James, but don't wait for him.

Some of the work trucks have started to pull away, but the jimadors that are left at camp rush to form a wide circle. From the middle of that circle, another scream rises up—belonging to a girl, I realize. I fear the worst: a girl attacked for access to her body, her clothing stripped off in the middle of camp in the bright, hopeful light of morning. There's grunting, snarling, whining—sounds that may belong to restless men.

Seeing something I don't, Leo curses and speeds ahead. He breaks through the mob of jimadors, and I follow. For a moment, all I see are shirts and arms. Then: dust. Then: a long, bare strip of flesh, a leg, some tatters of fabric, a horrific combination of blood mixed with dirt and the too-white shine of bone. That person—the pieces of that girl—is swirling through the dust, dragged along by a growling mass of gray flesh. It takes me a second to realize that the girl is Rosa, and that the roaring gray mass is one of the overseer's mastiffs. The overseer, however, is nowhere in sight.

"Stop!" I hear Leo cry out.

There's a flash of white light—the glint of a coa blade. Rosa's boyfriend, Ben, is standing over the fray, holding a tool high above his head, his eyes wild. Leo has his hand on the handle, preventing the downswing.

"You could hit her!"

He's right. Rosa is thrashing on the ground; so is the dog. And all the dust being tossed up makes it difficult to see either of them.

The jimadors have started hurling pewter plates and utensils at the dog, but those things, if they even hit, bounce off, making little to no impact. Leo kicks at the dog's flank, throws a punch at its massive, square head. Ben drops his coa, grabs on to the folds of the dog's skin, and tugs. Rosa's blood, at first pooling, is now thickly swirled in the dirt. Her bootless foot drags through it. Someone in the crowd spins away and throws up his breakfast.

I'm just standing there gawking, doing nothing. The last time I tried to do something, back in Truth or Consequences, I messed up. I can still hear James in the train, telling me it was foolish to step in and try to bend the path of fate. I'm no hero, but I hope there's someone here who is.

"Bruno," I whisper, scanning the crowd, and it's almost as if I will him into being. He runs from the direction of his bunkhouse, throwing on his button-up shirt. But when he sees what's happening, he strips the shirt back off and winds it around his hand. As he passes the campfire, he snatches up a cast iron skillet and charges up and through the crowd. He ratchets back his arm and brings the pan down full force against the dog's skull. There's a crack—more delicate than I would've thought, closer to an egg breaking than a tree limb splitting—and the dog falls heavy to the ground.

Bruno drops the skillet, then steps away. Ben dives toward Rosa, who's not screaming anymore. She's whimpering; her face has gone white. She mutters something and trembles. Ben's hands hover over Rosa's side, where the skin has been slashed. He wants to touch her, but he doesn't.

"I was just . . ." I hear Rosa say. "I wanted to . . ."

It's only now that James arrives, out of breath from sprinting, with the overseer right behind him. I can't see the overseer's eyes because of his sunglasses, but I can see the way his jaw twitches when he stares at his dog lying motionless in the dirt, its jaws and muzzle covered in blood, and then at Bruno.

"She must have done something," the overseer says. "My dog has never attacked anyone without permission before."

Someone in the crowd lets out a low hiss. *Without permission.*

James strips the shirt from his back, kneels, and presses the cloth to Rosa's side. I don't know how much good that'll do. I can see the gleam of a hip bone poking through ripped flesh. If her organs are lanced, she'll die in a matter of minutes.

There's no one to help Rosa, no healer to staunch the flow of blood or stitch up skin, but, still, James is trying. I look up and see Eva standing on the edge of the crowd, her eyes blazing, as if she delights in Rosa's pain.

Ben has his head dipped down. He is speaking to his girl in words so low no one else can hear. I don't even know if Rosa can hear. Her eyes are open, fixed to the sky; she's gasping and can't get air.

We are all quiet. We take off our hats and bring them to our hearts.

After several long minutes James rocks back on his heels and lowers his head. Rosa's eyes and mouth are still open, but she makes no sound. Ben starts wailing, and the overseer asks for volunteers to help carry away the body. She'll be put into the back of a truck, driven miles away, and buried in an unmarked grave. Some people believe that if a person is buried too close to camp, their spirit will find their way back, either out of loneliness or revenge.

Again, I don't offer my help. Rosa's body looks too much like Angus' did, sprawled and coated in dust. Their faces—mouths agape, eyes open wide—are almost interchangeable. It's Rosa. It's Angus. It's Rosa. I shiver, my spine like a thick length of twine pulled so tight it hums.

I wonder where Angus was buried. Far enough away so his spirit could settle? Or has he crossed mountains and desert to find me and ruin the Real Marvelous?

I wrap my arms across my chest and head back to the ranch house. No one sees me duck behind the closest building and throw up into a creosote bush.

TWELVE

I'M BACK IN the horse yard, rechecking Britain's straps, when Leo comes back up over the hill. Bruno trails a few steps behind him.

"Wait here," Leo calls out over his shoulder. "I'll find you a shirt."

Bruno is holding his right wrist with his left hand. He's wincing. A sheen of sweat has formed on his forehead. His hand is carelessly wrapped in his shirt, and I can see that it's covered in patches of raw, red skin.

"Don't move," I say, climbing onto Britain. I click my tongue and urge the horse out of the yard. "I'll be right back."

WHEN I STARTED working with the horses, Leo gave me a small pocketknife to use in case I need to cut rope or a thin strip of leather. As I ride, I pull it out of my pocket and scan the ground, hoping my memory serves me right. After I've gone almost a quarter of a mile, I spot it—a low, spiny bush, like a maguey in miniature. Aloe. I slow Britain, dismount just long enough for me to hack off a couple of spines from the plant, and then head back to the house, where Bruno is waiting in the stables, just as I asked. He's wearing a new shirt, one of Leo's most likely, and it barely fits over his broad shoulders.

I jump down from Britain and pass her reins to Leo. I take the plant and cut it lengthwise, like I'm peeling a carrot. A clear slime seeps out.

"Your hand," I command.

There, across his wide palm and up to the tips of his fingers, are white blisters, speckled against angry red skin. It must hurt like mad, but Bruno somehow manages to keep his hand from trembling.

I squeeze the aloe again, and the oozy liquid drops directly onto Bruno's skin. I move to rub it in with my fingers, but stop. "My hands are dirty."

Bruno tries to smile, but the pain transforms his expression into a scowl. "You think mine are any better? Go on."

As carefully as I can, I glide the liquid onto the burns, and repeat the process: slice, squeeze, glide, slice, squeeze, glide.

We are quiet. I take in Bruno's scent again: that sweet tobacco and maybe some cedar. I sneak glances at the tattoo across his chest, those scrolling cursive letters. I'd seen it, all of it, while he was running through the pack of jimadors toward Rosa and the dog.

Gone But Not Forgotten, it says. A tribute. I wonder who it's for.

Finally, Bruno clears his throat and asks, "Who taught you this?"

"My grandmother. She had some land. There were aloe plants. I saw one out here the other day when I was riding with Bell. It's supposed to make the burns feel better."

"It does. Thank you." A moment passes, and then Bruno lets out a long sigh. "It wasn't worth it."

I raise my head. Our eyes meet, and he goes on. "Rosa would've died anyway. The dog did too much damage before I even got there. Now I'm responsible for killing the overseer's pet."

I think to myself: *Tell him.* Tell him about Truth or Consequences, about the foreman and the dust storm, James and the ruse, That Time Outside Tulsa, Lane. Tell him because he is suffering right now, and he will understand.

"Sometimes you do things without thinking," I say. "In my experience those things are usually the right things. Not always, though."

He pauses, as if to consider my response, as if he knows it's coded and he's trying to figure it out. "Was this the right thing to do, Sarah?"

I lower Bruno's hand. I'm thrown, more than I should be perhaps, by the shortened version of my name. James is the only one who shortens my name, just as he's the only one who draws it out to its fullest.

"Everything okay here?"

Bruno and I both turn at the sound of James' voice. He's standing in the stable door, holding his blood-caked shirt in his blood-caked hand. There's a hard, dark edge to his expression.

"Sarah Jac was just working her magic with my burns," Bruno says.

"Yeah, she's good at stuff like that. I'm going to get cleaned up," James says before disappearing.

"Here." I hold out the other strips of aloe to Bruno, suddenly ready for this whole scene to be over. He takes them with his good hand. "Apply it as often as you can."

"Thank you. I will."

I wonder if he's waiting for me to say something profound because that's what sometimes happens in books and old movies when a person cares for another person. It's the point in the story where a heart cracks open and softness is revealed.

"I have to get back to Britain now," I say. "I'm late for Bell."

Bruno nods. His eyebrows knit together just slightly, and I think he might be disappointed in me.

I walk out of the stables and into the sun. I look for James, but he's gone.

LATER I LEARN that no one actually saw what caused the mastiff to go after Rosa, but there are theories, of course. Some say the dog trotted up to her during breakfast and sniffed at her plate. When she offered it a piece of pork, it latched on to her hand, pulled her to the ground, attacked her and never let go. Others say she was kneeling down, talking to the dog and stroking its head. Apparently, this was something she'd done often. I can imagine her doing it, given how attentive she's always been with her little mouse. Maybe she stood, made some sudden move, and spooked the dog.

There was also the theory—and this one was only repeated in whispers—that the dog had been bewitched. Sure, it was big, ugly, and snarling, but it had never been violent. Someone said its eyes had looked different that morning, glazed over. It went straight for Rosa, out of all the other jimadors, as if it were hunting her down, specifically, as if she had something it wanted.

What we know for sure is this: at some point after Rosa's death, Ben walked off toward the mountains. No one saw him in the fields. He was not back for supper, or in line for a coa the next day.

The desert took him, which is probably just what he wanted.

THIRTEEN

JUST AS EVA first appeared from the direction of the mountains, so do the wagons. I see them one morning as Bell and I are out with Britain. They move slowly, heavy transport pulled by twin black horses. People walk alongside them, at least half a dozen. As the wagons get closer, I notice that some of the people carry rifles; others carry oddly shaped black backpacks or quivers full of arrows. One woman carries a bundle against her chest that might be a baby. The people are all lean, their skin dark and tough from sun. Their pace is strong and steady despite the heat and all the weight they must be carrying. Bell and I watch, sipping water from our waterskins, as the wagons cut through the fields in the direction of camp.

"I'm not imagining this, right?" I ask.

"No," says Bell. "They've come before. They're pretty nice."

"Are they tinkers?"

Bell rotates in the saddle, and the brim of her hat whacks me in the chin. She squints, confused.

"Tinkers," I repeat. "Do they buy and sell and trade stuff? Is that what the wagons are for?"

"Sort of. But that's not all they do. They also put on a show."

I wasn't all that curious about Eva when she arrived, practically emerging from the earth itself. But these people. They came from somewhere. They're *going* somewhere. There's something hopeful in that.

The night promises to be full of magic, the good kind that makes us forget about girls dying in the dust, our injuries, our tainted food and lingering dehydration headaches, and allows us a break from thinking about the past or the future, or constantly brushing our fingers against the talismans that hang from some of our throats. Everyone—all the workers, all the foremen, the overseer, his remaining dog—has gathered to watch the show. Leo is here, sitting on a rail tie next to Raoul, the guy who attacked him that night at the bonfire. Fair-weather friends, I guess. Bell is also here, standing on the side of camp closest to the house. Farrah is beside her, and James is beside Farrah. For the past few days, he's worked late at the house and hasn't been at supper.

The musicians take their places. There's a young female drummer, a middle-aged male trumpeter, and an older woman who plays the violin. I haven't seen a violin since I left mine at my grandmother's, and that one was terrible compared to this woman's. On mine, the wood was warped and splitting. It needed oil and new strings. Its bow needed replacing or, at the very least, rosin.

Mine had a name, though. Its name was Might. As in, "Might makes right." Lane came up with that.

I rub my palms together and then trace the pads of each finger on my left hand with my thumb. My violin callouses are still there, layered under coa callouses and horse-rope callouses and whatever-else callouses.

Everyone quiets as the musicians begin a spooky and suspenseful tune. The notes start out faint and quiet, few and far between, slowly getting louder and more crammed together. Then the notes start to crash against one another, scraping and overlapping. The drummer hits her cymbal again and again, and the violinist drags out odd, discordant sounds. The mastiff starts howling, and the coyotes in the far, far distance catch on. I glance to Bell, and see her press the palms of her hands to her ears. Her mouth is open in a perfect little circle. She looks like a cartoon character, and I can't help but smile. My smile falters slightly when my eyes slip over to James and Farrah. Their hands are down by their sides. They aren't touching, not really, but they are very close, the kind of close that produces a wild current.

The music starts to lose its energy, like it's tired after a race, until it stops altogether. The howling stops, too.

Then the actors step onstage.

But it's not a stage. Not really. An old sheet, painted to represent a cityscape at night, hangs from the side of one of the wagons. All the dark buildings are outlined in different colors to mimic the neon lights. There are advertisements painted on the sides of the buildings, for things like soda and hospitals. Cities used to look like that.

The story is a romance. Simple really, but it's the simplest stories that always so thoroughly break my heart. There's a boy and girl. They fall in love. The problem is, the girl is dying. Together, she and the boy try to find a way to keep her alive, but her death, she's been told, is inevitable.

The actor playing the dying girl is amazing. Her fear is so real. At first, she's determined to fight. Eventually, however, she resigns herself to her fate. At the very end, her determination kicks in again. She's gasping, desperate for more breaths, and I know that all of us watching must be thinking of Rosa. We're hoping for the same thing: maybe, just maybe, she'll make it.

But, of course, she doesn't. The boy puts his ear to her chest and sobs. For a moment, we all sit in stunned silence. I look to Farrah, expecting to see the shine of tears in her eyes, because, out of all the people gathered here, she must know that girl's fear of dying and her desperate clinging to life, but her face is impassive. One of her hands, though, rests on her little sister's shoulder, and I watch her give it a squeeze.

Then someone in the audience sniffles, and the spell breaks. Together, we clap our blistered and calloused hands. We shout. We stamp at the dirt like horses. A wide-brimmed hat gets passed around, and we throw in what we can spare for a tip. For me, that's a half-dollar, which I'll probably regret tomorrow. My gaze travels to the edge of camp, and there's Odette. She isn't shouting or clapping. She's quiet and still. She's staring at James, who is leaning toward Farrah, brushing back a strand of her copper hair and whispering something in her ear.

With that gesture, Odette and I both know that something has happened. It happened in the handful of days since I last saw James in the cool kitchens of the Gonzales house. He's now convinced of my plan, the plan to move in on Farrah. Maybe he saw something; maybe he found something.

Whatever it is James says causes Farrah to laugh, high and bright. I look away, scanning camp for a distraction. The crowd has started to thin. The foremen all trudge back to their section of camp, and the night guards take their stations. One of the house workers guides Bell away. Some jimadors make their way through the dark to the bunkhouses. Others, like Leo and Raoul, set to work rebuilding the bonfire for those not yet willing to succumb to sleep. Bruno's nearby, watching because he can't offer help, his large arms crossed over his wide chest, his gaze serious and focused on the growing fire. His injured hand is wrapped in burlap.

I weave through the crowd in his direction. As I approach, he sees me and smiles.

"How's your hand?" I ask.

"Better. The aloe helps. It's hard to work with it wrapped up, though."

We pause for a moment, neither of us knowing what to say.

"You're not going back to your bunkhouse yet, are you?" I ask.

"I wasn't sure. Do you want to stay up for a while?"

Yes. The answer is yes. This night has my nerves buzzing and my skin feeling like it's shimmering.

"Did you know I play the violin?" I blurt.

"I did not." His smile gets wider. "Where did you learn how to do that?"

"I'm mostly self-taught. I haven't played in a long time, though."

Bruno nods his head in the direction of the wagon. "That must have just brought out a lot of memories then."

I make a noise, something between a sigh and a huff, before following the direction of Bruno's gaze, the place where the musicians played, holding us all in thrall. James is there, leaning over the now partially dismantled drum kit, holding out a coin and chatting with the drummer. After a moment, the drummer hands over one of her sticks and palms the coin. James straightens up, beaming, and faces camp.

"What's he doing?" I hear Bruno ask.

"I don't know."

"Your attention!" James calls out. "If I could have your attention for a moment!" Some of the jimadors stop and shift their focus to James. Some ignore him. Some call out colorful curses. James goes on without missing a beat because that's what James does.

"Come on up here, young lady," he says.

The *young lady* to whom James is referring is Farrah. If it were Odette, she would duck her head and act coy, but Farrah does no such thing. Instead, she marches up out of the crowd and takes her place next to him. She checks her posture—delicate shoulders thrown just slightly back, chin tipped just slightly up. She'd be the paragon of the proper, stoic lady if it weren't for the grin she's obviously biting her tongue to fight back. She doesn't sway tonight. She can stand on her feet just fine.

James holds up the drumstick. "Five cents says I can't hit this stick with my knife from this young lady's mouth from fifteen paces."

For a moment or two, there's silence.

"I'll take those odds!" Leo shouts, winding his way through the crowd. He stops in front of James and deposits a nickel at his feet. "This young lady is a blue-blooded chicken, and James here has some of the worst aim I've ever seen. He can barely cut the spines off a maguey. And those things don't even have legs."

I laugh, just barely, at one of the oldest cons in the book. I don't know how much steel Farrah has in her spine, but James' aim has always been true. Even in the dark. Even at fifteen paces.

James leans in and says something to Farrah. She opens her mouth just enough for James to slide the tip of the stick between her teeth, which results in several vulgar hoots from the jimadors.

"Ooh, remember not to get scared and bite too hard," Leo says loud enough for everyone to hear, eliciting another round of laughter.

More people shoulder through the growing crowd in front of James, and a small pile of coins starts to form at his feet. I lose count of the total, but I know that it's way more than James and I ever got when we did this trick together.

James crouches down and pulls his knife from his boot. Even in the dark, its white-bone handle gleams. He counts off fifteen steps and does an about-face. The crowd waits, expectation etched on their faces. They look to James, then Farrah, then back to James. They want something from him, and a part of me thinks it's not that they want him to hit the stick, despite the pile of coins indicating otherwise. They all know who this *young lady* is, and they'd bet a nickel to see—by *accident*—her cheek flayed open or the tip of her nose sliced off.

Odette, too, has worked her way to the front of the crowd. She leans to one side, favoring her injured foot. She's looking to James, silently pleading for him to notice her, but he doesn't. I bet Odette would pay more than a nickel, that she'd sacrifice larger chunks of her flesh, to see Farrah struck down right before her eyes.

"Can he do this?"

I startle. I was so fixated on James that I forgot Bruno is still next to me. "He won't miss. He never does."

James pulls back his arm, quick like always, and releases. This is a view I've never seen: knife spinning through the air, end over end. The blade smacks the wood of the stick, causing it to splinter. It breaks nearly in half before it's pulled entirely from the soft grip of Farrah's teeth. There's a gasp from the crowd, meager applause, and a loud, exaggerated curse from

Leo. James stoops to pick up his coins from the dust, a smile on his face.

When we do that trick—*every single time* we do that trick—my heart is beating like mad. I know James will never miss, but I worry. I worry about *myself*. What if, for some reason, I take a sudden step, or cough, or sneeze, or something in the far distance catches my attention? Each time, after James' blade goes whizzing by, it takes me a moment to get my heartbeat even, to loosen my nerves.

Farrah, though, just stands there, ever calm. She doesn't have her hand on her chest to confirm the beat beneath. Her eyes aren't widened, stunned that she's cheated injury or worse. When the steel of James' blade hit the wood inches from her face, she didn't even flinch, and her eyes, they never closed. Her lids never fluttered.

"Brave girl." There's admiration in Bruno's tone.

I want to disagree, but I can't.

Odette steps closer to James just as he stands from collecting his winnings. She says something I can't hear, and his resulting smile is forced. He puts his hand on her arm, squeezes once, releases her, and then turns away.

Odette drops her head, and my heart pinches in sympathy. I know that gesture and its total lack of feeling. It kills me sometimes, how good an actor James can be.

FOURTEEN

I'M ONE OF the first ones up and moving the next morning. The mess kids are just starting to throw hunks of chopped mesquite wood in a pile to make the fire. This early, the sky is divided: near the horizon it's pale blue, up higher it's ink black. It's cold without full sun.

Some of the troupe members are also awake, fixing up their horses, packing their wagons, or just milling about, waiting. The violinist is sitting on a low stool, wrapped up in a wool blanket. She lifts her head when she hears me approach. Her coil-curly hair was once very dark, but it's now shot through with gray. I don't want to stare too long, but I could swear her eyes are different colors: one black, the other light blue. They are two-toned, just like the morning sky.

She pokes at the small fire she's tending with a stick. "Can I help you?"

"I was wanting to go through your goods," I say. "Maybe make a trade."

"You have anything of value on you?"

"Depends."

The woman makes a dismissive little wave, giving me permission to climb into her wagon and hunt through her junk.

A tinker's wagon consists of treasures and trash: dolls; doll *parts*; wrappers from old candy, pressed smooth and flat; books; books with no covers; *just* covers with no books—mostly pulp and romance novels, featuring drawings of sultry women with hair and clothes in various states of disarray; coffee mugs boasting the names of diners and companies I've never heard of; cables and cords all wound into knots the size of my head; buckets of charms, coins, keys, what look to be small bones, buttons, and pins; and, strung up above my head, dozens—maybe hundreds—of origami birds in all different colors.

I crouch, riffling through a bucket of baubles and coins, until I find one I like, one that's not too scratched or dulled: it's a gold circle, about the size of a silver dollar. A hole is punched through it, close to one edge. Etched onto its face is a boat, its prow tilted slightly upward and its sails full of wind as it bounces across choppy water. On the flip side is a place name, partially obscured: ---*ster, Massachusetts.*

I grin. James and I don't give each other gifts very often, but this is perfect—something to keep in the pocket of his shirt, near his heart, to remind him of our grand plan of going East.

I stand, my head knocking against something. I push aside the paper birds and see the violin. It's used, obviously—there are wear marks around the chinrest and on the fingerboard—but the strings seem alright, and the hair on the bow that hangs next to it isn't completely frayed. All in all it's a good instrument, begging to be played. I don't know if I'll ever really play again, but I remember the thrill I got when I first received my violin, when it was laid across my two open palms.

With the violin and James' little ship charm in my hands, I jump down from the wagon. The woman is still at her fire, though now she's focused on a pot of boiling water.

I set my wares down in front of her and pull my bandanna from my waistband. I shift away in the attempt to hide its contents, but the woman is quick. She stands, leans over my shoulder, and picks at the chain of one of the necklaces.

"This one," she says.

I nudge her hand away. "Not that one."

"Yes, that one. Those other necklaces are cheap, and I don't want any of your dirty field coins."

Lane's necklace is the thing she wants. It's the one that shines the brightest, the one with the most delicate gold wire twisted into coils, and studded with tiny flecks of blue topaz. It is the last physical thing I have of hers, and I swear when I hold it in my hand, I can smell the bitterness of the tall grass that we used to lie in side by side in the summers all those years ago.

Camp is now fully waking up. I hear the mastiff barking and the shuffling of more feet. The wind picks up. The smell of horse and unwashed bodies pours out of the woman's clothes, wiping out my scent-memory of Lane in the grass.

I miss my sister, but she's long gone. I could hold on to her necklace forever, but that'll never bring her back. What's important is the future: my and James' future together.

I hand over the necklace, and before it can even glint once in the rising sun, the woman has tucked it into her pocket. She sits back down on her stool and adds coffee grounds to the now-boiling water. I assume the woman and I are finished. I gather my things and turn to go, but then I hear her ask: "Did you come from Truth or Consequences?"

My hollow stomach twists.

"Pale blue shirt," she says, stirring the grounds. "Mixed blood. Dark hair. Taller than average."

"That could be lots of people."

"Carries jewelry and her money in an old white bandanna in her waistband." The woman pauses. "We came from there not too long ago, three weeks maybe. They told us to keep an eye out. There's a reward."

I make a move that's too sudden, and the woman holds up her hand. It's marked with callouses, though hers tell me she's never done fieldwork. "I don't care about whatever happened," she says. "But *others* out there do, alright? Can I offer you advice?"

I'm silent, so she continues.

"If you were smart, you'd leave this ranch. We've been through a lot of places, and I can tell you that things here aren't right. There's talk of a witch."

I study this woman's dual-colored eyes. I guess there's no reason for her to lie. Maybe she's just trying to be helpful, or maybe she sees a younger version of herself in me.

Of course I want to leave the Real Marvelous, but that's not the easiest thing to do, now is it? Leaving requires money and careful timing. I can be quicker. I can cut more maguey. James can slide his way deep into Farrah's heart and her house, and work on scoping out its corners, on finding little things of worth that we can take with us when we go. When we go *soon*.

The woman glances at the violin I'm holding. "Can you play?"

"Yes."

"Well?"

"Yes."

"This camp is no place to hide," she says. "You can come with us. We're short-handed. We lost a girl last week, second violin."

I've never had much luck, so I've never had reason to believe in it. But the timing of this caravan coming to the Real Marvelous and the second violinist's death—that can't be anything but good fortune, as pure and lovely as reaching into a pocket and finding a forgotten dollar.

"I have a cousin," I say. "I can't leave without him."

I know what the woman's going to say before she even says it. There goes my luck, picked up and tossed. "There's only room for one."

"I'm sorry, then. But I appreciate your offer, and the warning."

I STASH THE violin in a dark corner of the stables, and that morning, for the first time ever, I'm in the very front of the coa line. I get a good tool, so sharp it's like the maguey cuts itself. I work hard all day. I don't get tired.

FIFTEEN

"YOU'RE UPSET."

It's been a full day and night since the travelers with the caravan put on their show, and Leo is helping me get Britain ready for her morning ride. "I don't see why. Bell obviously appreciated her gift."

Appreciated. Right. After I'd presented her with the instrument, she'd gasped, *For me?* Then she opened her mouth real wide and let out a scream so loud and high-pitched the dog down at camp started barking. It was possibly the first time I'd actually seen her happy—ecstatic, *exuberant*—as opposed to bricked up and guarded like she usually is. Bell then cradled the violin against her chest and disappeared inside the house so she could "hide it somewhere safe for later."

"My mood has nothing to do with Bell," I say, tightening Britain's girth.

"James then?" Leo asks. "He do something to tick you off?"

"I haven't seen James in a while." I avoid eye contact with Leo by pretending to struggle with one of the straps on Britain's stirrups. The ship pendant is still wrapped up in my bandanna, and I feel stupid carrying it around all the time, waiting. "So he hasn't been around to put me in a bad mood."

"Maybe the fact that he hasn't been around is exactly *what's* put you in a bad mood," Leo replies. From over his shoulder, I can see Bell emerging at long last from the house and trotting in our direction. Leo leans in and lowers his voice. "You know, you're not the only one here keeping a secret. He told me about your plans. About going East."

Leo's right. We all have secrets here, and we keep them hidden away the best we can, nested deep down, shoved into the mazes we've created inside ourselves. They are safe there.

"Sarah Jac," Leo says, attempting to read what I'm sure is a pinched and wary expression. "It's okay."

It's *not* okay. I don't know what Leo knows. He's being cryptic, and I don't like it. I've been feeling panicked and vulnerable ever since yesterday morning, when the traveler woman passed along her warning. That feeling has been multiplied by the fact that I haven't been able to find James and tell him about it. Now it feels like Leo has me backed into a corner. My mind jumps to what happened outside Tulsa. I have to stop this—cut this guy off, cut him out.

"I quit."

Leo blinks, takes a step back. Bell has come close enough to hear and stops in her tracks. She's confused, understandably.

"I don't want to work here with the horses or that girl anymore."

"Wait." He holds up his hands, palms facing me. "First of all, I don't think you have a choice about that . . ."

Leo is calling out my name, telling me to wait, that I have it all wrong, but I'm already gone, jogging back to camp in the direction of the coa line.

CUTTING MAGUEY WHILE I'm angry is good for me. It keeps me focused. So, all in all, I'm having a banner morning until Eva comes up during the water break and accuses me out of the blue of being a traitor.

That's what she says—that's *all* she says—as she glares at me: "Traitor."

I wait a second, thinking she'll go on, but she doesn't.

"What are you talking about?"

She sticks her finger in my face. I can see its callouses, its bluntly cut nail. "You're in cahoots with the family in the house."

"In *cahoots*?" I raise my tin cup to my lips and peer over Eva's head in the direction of the mountains. "Is that what you just said?"

"They want to destroy us. They work us to the bone and feed us rancid food. We've become *meat* for their *dogs*."

"Eva, save it for someone else, alright? You're wasting your breath."

She goes on, undeterred: "They want to destroy us, and you

140

are working with them. Teaching their daughter how to ride a horse, buying her *gifts*."

My gaze cuts down to Eva's. How would she know about that? She lifts an eyebrow, snickers. This is the Eva I hate most, not the one who stands in front of the campfire and shouts about omens, but the one who's quietly smug and acts all full of wicked wisdom.

The foremen blow their whistles. I toss down my cup and grab my coa. Eva has no idea how much I am not in the mood to deal with her this morning.

"I do what I want, Eva. For my own reasons."

I take a step to the side, but Eva grabs my wrist and wrenches it so my palm is facing up.

"Your life line is short," she says, pressing her gnarled thumb into my grimy hand. "You will die soon." She juts out her chin and nods. "This is good. This is good for you to know. It gives you the opportunity to decide how you want to live the rest of your brief life."

"Don't touch me." I yank my hand free and drag my palm against my jeans.

The foreman closest to us again blows his whistle. "Girls! Get moving."

Eva sneers at the foreman and then leans in toward me. "There will be a rebellion. You don't want to be on the wrong side."

"Make up your mind. There's a plague. There's a witch. Now there's a rebellion. I don't believe in your bullshit prophecies."

I march back to the rows and rows of uncut maguey and hear Eva's voice ring out: "You don't need to be a prophet to see what's coming. The signs are all around us."

IT'S MIDDAY WHEN a pickup truck pulls to a stop behind me and comes to an idle.

"Hey girl!"

It's the same man who took me to the house to meet Gonzales the first time. I don't even need to see his face to know it's him. I can hear how the cigar clamped between his teeth makes his voice sound thick.

I ignore him. He honks his horn. I ignore him, *again*. He honks his horn, *again*. He lays on the horn, and at that point, the jimadors around me stop and stare.

I hear the man get out of the car. He curses and grunts and slams the door. He better not touch me because I swear to God I will slice his arm off with this coa.

"Hey!" he calls out again, with a chuckle this time, like this is all some game he has total control over, like I'm not embarrassing him in front of his inferiors. "Girl. Get in the truck. I'm taking you back to camp."

The man grabs my right arm to twist me around, which wrenches my shoulder and causes me to drop my tool. The blade lands inches from my foot.

"You're going back to the house," the man growls.

I wince. The man notices how I've tensed up under his hand and digs his thumb deeper into my ball-and-socket joint. The pain—from an old injury that never healed right—is so sharp and bright, I'm momentarily blinded.

"That hurts?" the man asks. He leans in to where the tip of his cigar sizzles just a hair's breadth away from my cheek. I can hear it, too, that faint crackle of burning tobacco.

"No," I lie.

He grips me harder, and the muscles in my legs fail. The man takes that as an opportunity to toss my limp body into his truck. My head slams against the dashboard, and when I raise my fingers to a spot just above my hairline, they come away wet with blood. That wound hurts, but it hurts way less than the man's thumb pressed into my shoulder joint.

I cradle my arm and turn to look out the window as I'm driven away. Some of the jimadors are scowling at me. They assume that if one worker acts up, all will be punished. Others, like Bruno, hide smiles of admiration. He raises his hand to shield his eyes from the sun. I see it as a salute. The truck passes Eva and Odette. They're standing side by side. Eva's eyes are wide, full of pride, full of *I told you so.*

"What happened to your face?"

Bell is laughing as she asks this question. She tries to pull the laughter back into her mouth by covering it with her hand.

"I hit it," I say, staring at Leo until his gaze drops. "I hit it when I was thrown into a truck. That's what happened to my face."

This somehow makes Bell laugh even harder. Leo spits in

the dirt and says something about how I should've just been cooperative and not made a big deal of it.

Britain's still saddled up in the yard from earlier, but I head to the stables, where I yank the white horse's tack from the wall and haul it outside.

"You're on Britain today," I say to Bell. She stops laughing. "But. But . . . I . . . ."

"Shut up, Bell, and get on the horse!" Bell doesn't move. "Get on the damn horse. Leo. Help her up."

"Sarah Jac . . ." Leo starts.

"If she wants to learn how to ride, she's going to learn how to ride. No more babysitting."

I throw the blanket and saddle onto the white horse and glance at Bell. She's falling apart at the prospect of doing something on her own. Her pale skin goes paler. Her lower lip trembles.

Lane wouldn't have acted this way. Not ever. Lane was scared shitless all the time—*always* when we pulled some kind of scam—but she understood what it was like to have to do things that were scary and that you weren't proud of because that's how survival works. Aside from me, no one ever knew how scared she was. That's because I would always remind her what our grandmother told us: it's okay to be scared, but it's not okay to show it.

"What would you do if your mother was here, Bell?" I tighten the saddle around the white stallion's belly. He tosses his head and stamps. I'm making him nervous. "If she was here right now watching you, what would you do?"

Bell looks to her feet.

"What would you do?" I demand.

"This isn't helping," Leo says.

"Leo, do me a favor and shut up."

I repeat my question to Bell. "What would you do? You'd get up on the horse, wouldn't you?" I urge. "You'd prove you weren't a little chickenshit."

"Sarah Jac," Leo warns.

"Leo!" I shout. "Did you not *just* hear me tell you to *shut* up?"

"I'd get on the horse!" Bell yells.

I'm shocked. It sounds so much like a wolf cub trying to find its first howl, I'd bet she's never truly yelled before. Her gaze is still down at her feet, but her hands are balled into fists at her side. She's mad; I've made her mad. That's something.

"Then do it," I command.

Bell walks toward Britain, and Leo lifts her up so that she can grab the saddle horn and pull herself up and over. While Leo adjusts the stirrups for Bell, I finish up with the white horse.

"What's this horse's name?" I ask.

"King," Leo replies.

"King," I say, clicking my tongue. "Sorry about my mood. It's been one of those mornings."

I mount the white horse, and it's obvious he doesn't like me. I haven't given him much reason to. I've been aggressive with his tack and in my tone. He shuffles a bit, stepping back, stepping forward. I can feel his muscles tense, release, and tense again. I reach back up to the wound at my hairline. It's stopped bleeding, but it's still gummy to the touch.

"We're trotting today." I take King's reins and guide him toward the center of the yard. "Maybe up to a canter. But we'll just stay here and do circles in the yard. Britain knows you, so you don't have to be afraid of her."

"I want to go out," Bell says, adjusting her hat.

"Really?" Leo and I ask at the same time.

"I want to go out," Bell repeats, more forcefully this time.

"Fine," I say. "Let's go."

THE LANDSCAPE IS particularly stunning today. It must have something to do with the clouds being thicker or lower, but the mountains actually look farther away than normal, like they've been picked up and moved several miles to the west. They're hazy, not copper-dusted, as James would say.

We haven't reached a canter because Bell is stuck on the trot. At first she jostled around in her saddle with such turbulence I thought she might fall off Britain, but she soon got it down: eyes to the front, spine straight, belly in, legs firm. I even heard her laugh, chirping and bubbly like little girls are supposed to laugh. For near-on forty-five minutes she's been transitioning from a walk to a trot to a walk to a trot. She's gripping the reins too tightly because she's nervous, but despite that, she's never once pulled back too hard on them.

"I'm sorry I laughed at you," Bell eventually says.

"It's fine."

"Thank you again for the violin. I love it."

"Not a problem."

"Can I see you gallop?"

I pull my gaze from the mountains to Bell's chubby face. She's giving *me* a gift. I should take it.

"You want to see me gallop?"

Bell nods. "James said you can go fast."

"Let me take Britain," I say. "She knows me better."

I hop down from King and help Bell dismount, quickly in case she changes her mind. I give my hat to Bell to hold, show her how to grip the stallion's reins, close but not too close to his chin, and instruct her to stay just like that.

"I'm going down toward the mountains and then turning right back." I readjust Britain's stirrups and climb on. The horse's muscles shift underneath me, and I can barely hide my excitement. I've been waiting for this for weeks. As soon as I strike my heels into her sides, Britain takes off.

I remember immediately what it feels like to be on a horse when it's going full speed—the propulsion forward, the ripping force of wind—but I'd forgotten what it sounded like. There's the thunderous pounding of the hooves and the rush of air, but there's also silence—a noisy, full silence that comes from being alone with sounds made by the earth and wind and a living thing. That not-silent silence makes me want to ride forever, to the mountains and past them, across the deserts to the wheat fields, to the trees in the East, to the water.

"That's my girl!" I whoop. "That's my Britain!"

Being on this horse, it's overwhelming, all-consuming in the best, most magical way. In this moment—with Britain and the wind—I forget about all the things that have been chasing me: the dead foreman, the curses, the ghost of my sister. It's just me and Britain, and together we can outrun it all.

It's impossible to tell how far I've gone because of the unchanging landscape and the lack of physical markers, but it feels like miles. I imagine Bell peering out at the blurry horizon, diligently holding King, hot in the high sun and starting to worry.

Britain isn't tiring, but I can hear her breathing now and see her hair darkening with sweat. I slow down just enough to turn her, and we race back to King and Bell, who emerge as just specks in the distance. The hazy mountains are behind me. The heat beats down on my head. It really does: it beats. *Thump, thump.*

I'm so happy. Is it wrong to feel like I've deserved this happiness?

I dig my heels into Britain's side and whoop again.

Finally, finally. It's just me and her. She runs faster, just for me. My Britain.

SIXTEEN

LEO AND FARRAH are waiting in the yard. I scan for James, but he's not there. The slant of the shadows on the earth tells me that Bell, Britain, and I have been out too long. Even with her hat for protection, a rash of deepest pink is visible on an exposed patch of Bell's shoulder, where she's been cooked by the sun.

"You should have seen Sarah Jac!" Bell cries out. "She made Britain go *so fast*."

Leo is not impressed. He helps Bell dismount and immediately walks her horse over to the stables.

"What's his problem?" I ask Farrah, climbing down from King.

"He said you were mad when the two of you left. He was worried."

I can smell food—the earthy tang of boiled greens—being prepared down at camp.

"Who taught you horses?" Farrah asks.

"My grandmother. She had a farm."

For a moment, neither of us says anything. Farrah shifts her gaze over to the mountains and holds it there. That first time I saw the elder Gonzales sister out in the maguey fields on Britain I thought the expression on her face could best be described as *haughty*, and that she looked at the landscape like a proud, puffed-up owner would. I thought she admired the desert and the terrain the same way I admired the small, collected treasures stuffed in my bandanna. Now, I'm not so sure that's right. The way her yellow-tinted eyes are set on the mountains, it's like she's watching them, or looking *beyond* them, like she's been waiting patiently for so, so long for someone or something to appear from their far side. All of a sudden, I feel uncomfortable, as if I've stepped into a moment that's not mine.

"Well, then," I say. "Unless I plan on fighting for scraps, I need to head down to camp. I'm sure Leo will be back for King in a minute."

"Your farm," Farrah says, finally facing me, "was it like how farms are in books? With animals and a red barn and green rolling hills?"

"Something like that."

"Were there many trees?"

"When I was there last, people from the cities were starting to come in and cut them down, but yeah, up until then there were lots of trees."

"Do you plan to go back?" she asks.

I don't like to think about what my grandmother's land would be like now: stripped, fallow. Or the structures: dismantled for their wood, taken over by squatters who are probably wearing all my grandmother's old clothes and eating off her dishes.

"I'm sure there's nothing to go back to."

"That's too bad," Farrah says, and I believe she means it. "Do you miss it?"

"Not as much as I probably should."

Farrah holds my gaze, like she's urging me on, like she wants there to be something shared between us.

But then I remember Eva's words, slamming into me like wind. *They are trying to destroy you.*

"Excuse me," I say, stepping around Farrah, "I have to go."

I WAS RIGHT about the greens. They've been boiled to a paste and need salt, but someone in the mess crew thought to add cayenne pepper so that's a nice surprise. After shoveling them down, I head back up to the ranch house. I'm tired of waiting on James to come to me. I'll find him myself.

I figure the best place to start is the stables. When I'm at the door, I hear two people speaking in low tones. I walk inside, as quietly as I can, where a lamp is lit, and it's just bright enough for me to see two shadowed bodies sitting across from each other on the ground in front of the horse stalls. I see their hands, fingers stroking palms, like when James rubs his strong thumb against my aching muscles. He'll hold my wrist in place and stretch out my fingers. You have to know someone's body well to do that for them. You have to really care about them.

My eyes adjust to the dark, and I recognize Raoul. The top

few buttons of his shirt are undone. The bundle he wears on a string around his neck rests on his bare chest, directly above his heart. With him is Leo. I take what I think is a silent step back, but Leo immediately shifts. His eyes lock on mine. He smiles. It's a melancholy little thing, so different from what I'm used to seeing from him.

Raoul sees me next. He drops Leo's hand. His heart must have split a bit, like mine does whenever James and I are forced apart and our time together is stolen from us.

I understand, finally. Leo is running a con, just like us. That's what he was trying to tell me the other day.

"What are you doing here, Sarah Jac?" Leo asks.

"You . . ." I pause. "That fight—at the fire, weeks ago, between the two of you—that was staged. Did James know?"

Of course James knew. The fight was probably James' *idea*.

Leo is silent.

"I'm here for the horse," I say.

"The *horse*?"

"Britain. I was coming to check on her."

Raoul is gnawing at his thumbnail, watching me, strategizing. Strategizing what? Against *me*?

"Leo, we need to do something," he says.

"No," Leo replies, unwinding his long legs and rising to stand. "It's fine. Go back to the bunkhouse. I'll find you later."

Raoul curses and reluctantly gets to his feet. As he leaves, he pins me with a glare. He's angry and disappointed. I know so well what that feels like, so I can't blame him.

Once Raoul's disappeared into the night, Leo folds his arms across his chest and lowers his head. I've disappointed him, too.

"How long?" I ask.

Leo's head snaps up. "How long what?"

"How long have you known him?"

"Not long. We met on the train."

"Leo. I can go find him. Talk to him. Tell him I'm the last person . . ."

"Yes," Leo says, cutting me off. "The fight at the fire was staged. James helped."

"What about the first one? When your lip got split."

Leo shakes his head. "That was just me being stupid."

"Let me go talk to Raoul." I take a step back toward the door.

"Forget it. I'll find him and deal with this. You might as well stay. Be with your horse."

I wait for Leo to leave, but he doesn't. He just kicks at the dust with the toe of his boot, frowning.

"What?" I ask finally. "You're not worried I'll say anything about this, are you? Because I won't."

"I know you won't." Leo's response comes quick. "I'm debating whether or not I should tell you something I know will hurt you."

"If it's about James, just say it."

Leo takes a step forward. "Obviously, I know about the games you two play with people, Sarah Jac, because I've played them, too, and played them better. This time you might've made a mistake."

My hands clasp in front of me, in front of my heart. My thumb presses into my palm and drags across the swoop of my too-short life line.

"What does that mean?" I whisper. "What mistake?"

"It means that right now James is in the house with Farrah. He usually sleeps here in the stables, but he snuck in there to give me and Raoul some time together." Leo shrugs. "And to be with her, of course."

Of course.

"It's a ruse." My words snag in my throat. "We know what we're doing."

Leo cocks his head. "I don't know."

"She's dying."

"I don't know," Leo repeats. But there's a tone to his voice this time: pity. Leo pities me, and I can't stand it.

I hear something, the low hoot of an owl or the echo of a faraway train. But I can't help imagining it's a noise from the house: a low growl of pleasure from the depths of James' throat, a sound I miss so much it makes my chest burn.

Farrah, right now, could be bringing out that sound. His strong, sure hands could be traveling across the bare expanse of her skin and making her tense up and sigh out his name. He can make her feel like she could live forever.

"If you feel like waiting," Leo says, as he finally makes his way out the door, "by all means . . ."

Eva and the traveler woman and the man with the bad knee back at Truth or Consequences said that something was very wrong at the Real Marvelous. Eva predicted bad things to come, that order would be warped and flipped, that there would be sickness and pain. What if they were right? If James is with Farrah, maybe it isn't all my fault. Maybe it's the land, *this* land, and the lies that have built up and festered in it over the course of several centuries, just like Leo said that first night at the fire. There could be something wrong here, in this very dirt. And all that wrongness might be just about to bubble up, ooze from hacked maguey, or seep skyward through the deep, dry cracks in the ground.

We have to leave this place.

I can't be alone right now. King is quiet, but I can hear Britain letting out huffing, nervous breaths. I go over and grab one of the wool horse blankets, wrapping it around my shoulders because the night has gotten colder.

My horse is in the back of her stall, resting against a mound of hay. She snorts in greeting. I want to curl up next to her, but I give her space and sit down just inside the door. I bring my knees in to my chest and cover myself with the blanket. It's not a comfortable position, but after a while I fall asleep to the smell of horse and hay and the low, murmuring sounds of breath.

I wake only once, when I think I hear the stable door swing open. But it was nothing—a dream, perhaps.

SEVENTEEN

JAMES APPROACHES AS I'm readying Britain for the morning ride. He has no idea I spent last night waiting for him in the stables. He's smiling that ragged, marvelous smile of his. I hope I'm the reason for his smile, that he's happy to see me, but I wonder if the true reason is the fresh memory of his long night in Farrah's room.

"It's been a while," I say, brushing down Britain's coat.

"It has. So what's new?"

I pull out the charm from my pocket, but my gaze catches on James' collar. There's a pin there, one I've never seen before. It's a tiny flag, the proud symbol of a place I don't know and that may not even exist anymore. Standing out against a center white stripe is the silhouette of a palm tree.

"It was a gift," James says. "Odette gave it to me."

"Because she knows how much you love trees."

James doesn't reply. Like me, Odette must have seen the tinker's wagon, and her thoughts went to James. She carefully combed through the woman's wares, hoping to find the perfect, most meaningful thing. I wonder what Odette traded for this pin. I wonder if she, too, has small treasures stashed on her person. Did she have a piece of jewelry from a dead little sister that she swore she'd never part with until she met a beautiful boy with moss-green eyes and a smile full of mischief and promise?

"Why are you wearing it?" I ask. "Now, with you and Farrah . . . why would you still string Odette along? It's . . ."

Cruel, I want to hurl at James like he once hurled at me. It's cruel. Instead I leave the sentence unfinished.

James shrugs and then reaches up to rub the surface of the pin with his thumb. "She seemed so excited to give it to me. It was the other morning, after the travelers came through. I never made any promises to Odette, so it's not like I'm breaking some kind of sacred vow between us."

"She won't see it that way," I say.

"No. She probably won't."

I take James' hand and slap the charm in his palm.

"For you."

James flips it over, smiles at the sight of the boat. "Where did you get this?"

"One of the travelers—a woman—had a wagon full of stuff. That's probably where Odette got her pin. Do you like it?"

"Of course," James replies. "*How* did you get it?"

I ignore his question. "The woman who sold it to me also said I look a lot like a girl who killed a foreman in Truth or

Consequences, which means we should think about leaving, right? She said there's a reward out."

James shakes his head, brushing off my concern. "I haven't heard any rumors like that. Besides, we can't leave now. We don't have enough money."

I try to protest, but he stops me by saying my name, *Sarah* . . . all drawn out. He looks past my shoulder to the fields, which makes me feel stupid and small.

I check to see that no one's around and take James' hand. I miss its roughness and warmth. I run my thumb over his palm just like Raoul did to Leo last night and try to avert my eyes from the bright sunlight reflecting off his pin.

"We have to leave this place," I say. "I think there's something really wrong here."

He gives me a smile—not so ragged and marvelous this time—then squeezes my hand and releases it.

"You're worrying too much." He shifts his weight, right foot to left. "Listen, though. Sarah. I'm going to be gone for a while."

I step back. "Gone where?"

"The family's going to El Paso for business, and Gonzales has asked if I'll come along."

"Since when do business transactions require groundskeepers?"

"It's not that. I'm just . . . he told me they need a hand. He said he'd pay me extra. So, it'll be a good thing, right?"

I hate the way he makes it into a question. *Right?* There's so much blame in that little upticked word. It's like he's forcing me to agree or else I'm being irrational.

"Is Farrah going?"

"She'll meet us there. Not Bell, though. Farrah's going to see a doctor and get some treatments, and they don't want her sister around for that."

"Don't." I grab his hand again. He's still holding the pendant, and I press it deeper into his palm. "Don't go. Just stay. Or leave with me. I have a little money. We can go today. *Now.* We can take Britain, ride her to the rails and wait for a train. You can't just leave me here alone."

"You're the strongest person I've ever met, Sarah Jac. You can survive a few days without me."

"Please," I whisper. "James, please."

I wait, pleading in silence, but James just looks at me, sadly I think, his eyes so vibrant in the morning sun.

"I have to go," he says, sliding his hand from mine. "I'm expected at the house."

I'M STARING AT the stars. Out here in the desert, you don't even really have to tilt your head up to see the sky. The sky is all around. It's practically all there is. And it's not that the stars are bright, like in the lullaby. They're simply everywhere. They pierce and poke the black. They pierce and poke me. I feel like I'm leaking.

Leo nudges me, and I blink.

"Lost your appetite?" he asks.

We worked late tonight, cleaning out the stables, and barely made it down to camp in time for supper.

I glance down to the plate balanced on my knees. A couple of flies bounce across a gray glob of gristly meat. I make no move to shoo them away.

I look back to the sky. If I stare at the stars, then I don't stare at the ranch house. Its lights are ablaze, which is uncommon for this time of night. Silhouettes move across the windows. The people inside—James, Farrah—must be up late, getting ready to leave.

"Do you think they're trying to destroy us?" I ask.

"No." Leo stabs at his dinner. "If they destroy us, who will cut their maguey?"

"That's not what I mean." I set my plate on the ground and cross my arms over my chest, suddenly cold. "I'm talking about our hearts. If they destroy our hearts, our *spirits*, our bodies will still keep working. I've seen it."

Leo snorts. "Your *spirit* is just fine."

An indistinct shout rises up from the direction of the ranch house, followed by what sounds like the door of a truck slamming shut.

"Have you thought about leaving the Real Marvelous?" I ask.

Leo's response comes quick: "Yes."

"Would you leave without Raoul?"

He shrugs. "Probably. Maybe. I haven't known him as long as you've known James. We don't have the history you two have. It's easier."

"Is it?"

He smiles, chewing. "That's what I tell myself."

"I'm sorry about what happened last night. I really am."

Leo picks my plate up off the ground, stacks it on top of his, and stands. "I know," he says. "Good night, Sarah Jac."

I wait, staring at the stars, even though they continue to pierce and poke. I'm waiting for James, of course. I'm holding in that small bit of hope that wants to seep out. Maybe he'll have a change of heart. Maybe he's up there at the house, desperate to get to me, to put his hands on me, to give me his smell.

He never comes.

THE BEES COME, though, two days after James leaves the Real Marvelous, in the afternoon when the sun is at its highest point and when we are at our most tired. One lands on my wrist, feels its way around, and then circles away. The guy cutting next to me slaps himself on the neck and curses. I watch him hobble backward. He drops his coa and begins batting himself as if he's just realized he's on fire. Something zings past my ear. Someone down the line screams. Up and down the row, coas hit the ground.

Then I hear it: a rising and a falling, like thousands of voices all trying to find the right note. I turn east and see a wide, opaque cloud across the sky, but it's not a dust storm, not this time. Dust storms are orange and make a roaring sound. This cloud is like static, dotted black, and isn't moving with the wind, but like it's *made* of wind.

One of the bees lands on my thigh. I swat it away, but another immediately takes its place. Farther down, two bees tiptoe across my shoelaces, probing for the sweet maguey sap that coats my boots.

A trio of young jimadors runs past me. They're carrying a woman whose cheek has swollen to the size of an orange. She's clutching her throat and wheezing.

Finally, one of the bees gets me: on my back, up near my shoulder blade. I reach around, slap the spot instinctively, and am stung again. I'm unsettled less by the stabs of pain than by the knowledge that a bee has worked its way past two layers of clothing. I drop my coa, shrug off my button-up, untuck my cotton shirt, and watch the trapped insect fly out and hover in front of my face. In my peripheral vision, I can see another land on the brim of my sun hat. Several have burrowed into my hair and have started to explore.

The hum of the bee cloud gets louder, rising into a thunderstorm howl. The sky begins to pulse black. The horses are shrieking. The foremen are steering them around toward camp and breaking into runs. I run, too.

The diesel trucks are parked in a row almost a hundred yards in front of me, and one already is pulling away. Several of the jimadors are in the process of jumping into its open back. Others are close behind, crying out for it to stop.

I get stung on my hand, on my cheek. People scream. I don't. I'm afraid that if I open my mouth the bees will rush down my throat. I see Raoul, running in front of me. He trips and falls, and when I skid to a stop to help him, someone elbows me in the kidney and shouts at me to get out of the way. I grab Raoul's hand. He screams and wrenches it away. A bee flies out from between our palms. I reach out for him again and catch his necklace, the talisman made from sticks and twine. He twists away, and the string snaps. I try to pull him up, but he slugs me in my bad shoulder.

I stumble back and notice that another truck has started to pull away. It's full, but still some people try to jump in only to be knocked right back out. There aren't enough trucks. The three that remain or are just about to leave are packed, but the one that took off first is not. It's far away, and its bed is only half full.

"Get away from me!" Raoul yells.

This time I decide not to stand in the way of fate. I leave him and run.

A girl who can't be older than eleven pulls a grown woman to the ground by her braid. A man jabs at another with the blade end of his coa. I pass Bruno, and call out his name just as he shoves another jimador into the spines of an uncut maguey and stomps straight down on his knee to keep him from getting to a truck. He stares at me, panting, and the expression on his face—that determination, that *hate*—I could never have imagined him looking that way.

"Go!" he shouts.

So I go.

Soon the ground is littered with bodies that are either twitching or completely still. Some of those bodies are swollen. Others have gashes in their necks: wounds from coa blades. The bees dance across their eyelashes, and their tiny feet dip into wounds.

I break into an even harder sprint and gain some ground. I can run fast for a long time across this dry, rocky soil, but I'm starting to feel shaky and delirious, either from the sun or the stings. Twenty or so yards in front of me, the truck quivers and shakes; it kicks up dust.

On the other side of that dust, the jimadors in that truck stare at me dispassionately. Not one of them is leaning out the back, extending a hand for me, urging me forward. I shouldn't be surprised. Aside from the rare exception, we don't really help one another here. We wait for weather or disease or bees or a sudden accident to come and pick one another off so we can prove to ourselves that we're more worthy than someone else to be alive. I'll be damned if I give anyone that satisfaction.

With another push forward, I'm able to grab the side of the truck bed and pull myself in. For a moment, I just lie there, sweating, shaking, and staring at the bright sky. Another bee buzzes in my ear, and I lazily slap it away.

A face appears to hover over mine. It's blurry, doubled. For a moment I think it's James, but then I remember that James is gone. I blink and see that the face belongs to Eva. She's hatless.

And smiling. The sun shines down from behind her, giving her a halo. She looks like Farrah did that morning in the kitchen, like an illustration, like something out of a story. She puts a warm palm across my forehead. I push it away.

"You were spared," Eva says. "This is a beautiful thing."

EIGHTEEN

THERE'S SOMETHING WRONG with Britain. I stumble down from the truck and see her in the yard, kicking and thrashing. I try to reach her, but I'm tripping over my own feet, thick-tongued and delirious.

When I get closer, I see the welts: on her neck and on her legs. One of her eyes is swelled nearly shut. She's squealing in pain.

"James!" I cry out, instinctually, before I'm able to catch myself. "Leo!"

There is no Leo, but Bell is there, up on the fence, leaning over the top rail and crying out for the horse.

"What's wrong with her?" she shrieks.

"Inside!" I shout. "Get inside!"

There are no bees here, but I can still hear them, if only in my head—the eerie orchestral swell.

"I brought out Britain," Bell says between sobs, "and she ran away."

"You brought her out by yourself?" My head is throbbing, and I'm suddenly so tired. I just want to sit, just for a minute. I grip the fence to keep myself standing. It's then I notice a welt, the size of a hunk of coal, on the top of my hand.

"Why would you bring her out by yourself, Bell?"

"You weren't here!" she cries out. "And I couldn't find Leo."

"Where is Leo? Bell, think, please."

"I don't know!" Her sobs have started to sound like moans. "I don't know! I'm sorry. I didn't mean to hurt her."

"Where is Leo?"

"I don't know!"

"Go inside!" I command. "Go now!"

I run to the stables. Leo's cot is there; his things are there. King is in his pen, anxiously shuffling and snorting.

Britain's screams take on a different pitch, drawn out and shrill. I run back to the yard and see her on her back, twisting on the ground. Her eyes are wide and lolling, positioned straight up to the glaring sun. Her tongue is hanging out of her mouth, dragging half circles in the dirt.

That's when I notice her front leg. It's reaching toward the sky but at an awkward angle. It's a twig, snapped in half but dangling by the thinnest fiber. Britain rolls to her side, tries to get up, and then collapses under the pressure.

I'm in so, so much pain. I can feel the stings all over my body, but they aren't simple stings. Those tiny pricks are just the center of a much larger circle of radiant pain.

"Leo." My voice cracks on his name. I'm crying. I'm crying as

I head back to the stables and over back to Leo's cot. I grab the rifle and check that it's loaded. Someone else could do this—the overseer, or one of the foremen—but I want it to be me.

"Stupid horse!" I shout as I go back into the yard. "Britain, you stupid horse!"

Stupid horse, that James led me to that night when we first arrived here. Stupid horse, that I slept next to and pretended was mine. Stupid horse, that I went tearing off into the desert with. Stupid horse, that escaped, ran straight into a swarm of bees, and then broke her leg on her way back.

I have a flash of magical thinking, that maybe I can heal her, with time and with my love. She's young, right? Strong and healthy. But no. That leg is destroyed. It'll never be right again. She's still twisting, but she calms a little when she sees me approaching. I glance over the camp. More trucks are coming back from the fields. The workers are pouring from the backs and shouting for help.

What is happening here? We are all breaking. We are broken.

I look to make sure Bell isn't around. Then I press the two barrels of the gun into the welt above Britain's eye and pull the trigger.

THE NEXT DAY is devoted to burials. The workers go out early and pile the bodies in the backs of the trucks and take them miles away from the maguey fields and out past the trash heaps. If there are any personal effects, the workers take those from the bodies, so the dead can be identified by a friend or relative at camp, if they have a friend or relative. Most will remain anonymous.

The day after that, there are executions. The dozen or so jimadors who were accused of inciting violence during the bee swarm, of turning their fists or their coas against one another or, worse, the foremen, are given the briefest moment to pronounce their innocence before they are blindfolded and shot, right in the middle of camp. Among those put to death is Bruno. He stood there, hands behind his back, and remained perfectly and completely silent, even as the foremen raised their rifles.

Or so I'm told. I'm spared the sight of the burials and executions because I'm confined to my cot with fever.

I'm past crying and on to something else that feels worse. I don't remember much after putting Britain down. I don't remember the sound of the shot, but I do remember the kick of the rifle against my shoulder. I think I fell down. I remember being in my cot, stripped down to my tattered underwear. Eva was sitting next to me, skimming a brown-shelled egg across my arm. It's a folk remedy, a way to draw out bad spirits from beneath the skin and trap them in the shell.

I remember trying to push her away. I didn't want her to know how much bad stuff had soaked into my skin.

"Don't touch me," I said, but she wouldn't stop.

I remember mumbling, "Where's my money?" and Eva knowing exactly what I was talking about. She reached underneath my pillow and pulled out the edge of my bandanna so that I could see it.

"You believe now."

This was not a question, and I didn't reply.

Eva continued to run the cold eggshell across my forehead, and I went back to sleep, wondering where on earth she got that egg.

I wake again when I hear Eva announce that I have a visitor. It's Farrah. I'm sure I'm imagining her. I thought she was gone, too, like James—to El Paso with her father. The fact that she's not with James makes my heart skip. I'm hurting, but I'm happy. Farrah's not wearing blank white, like usual; she's in denim, a chambray shirt and jeans. There's a tiny stain of something at her knee. It seems so strange to see her dirty, even if just a little bit.

Imaginary or not, I don't want her here, but I can't tell her that. She takes a seat on the edge of my cot and pulls something out of the small satchel she's brought along with her.

"I have something for you," she says. "From Bell."

She holds out a single red button looped around and around with thin wire.

"It's for protection." Farrah's voice sounds so light, like air, like music.

I can't imagine that she's ever raised her voice or laughed so loud and for so long that her throat has become hoarse. What kind of life must that be like?

"The button is supposed to be you," she goes on to explain, "and the wire wrapped tight is there to keep you safe. My mother believed in things like this, little tokens and talismans.

She used to stuff our pockets full of these buttons and bundles of herbs to either bring good luck or ward off evil. She taught Bell and me how to make them when we were little, even the bad luck charms made of teeth and bone. I'd forgotten all about it, honestly, but Bell has recently started stashing them around the house."

"Your mother?" I ask.

"She was from out here. The desert."

Farrah glances up at the silent, watchful faces of the other girls and women in the bunkhouse.

While she's studying them, I'm studying her: trying to puzzle her out. If Leo was right, and James really does want to be with her, then there have to be reasons why. Is it that long swoop of her chin, or the fact that her fingernails aren't crusted with grime? Is it her musical voice and the way in which everything she says seems so composed and considered?

I turn my head. It hurts. I'm trying to find Odette, but I can't.

Farrah again reaches into her satchel, and this time pulls out a brown glass vial.

"A couple drops under the tongue every morning and night," she says, putting both the vial and the button in my sweaty hand. "It helps with headaches."

"Thank you," I say. "Tell Bell I'm sorry about Britain. Leo, too. Tell him I tried to find him, but couldn't."

"We can't find him, either," Farrah replies. "No one's seen him since yesterday morning—before the bees arrived. His things are all still in the stable. It's possible he was out cutting maguey and his body's still out in the fields, and no one's found it yet. We're short-staffed now, especially with James gone with Papá. You're expected back at the house when you're well. My father always insists that even during our most trying times, we do our best to keep order."

"*Trying times?*" Eva growls, pouncing on Farrah. "Do you think that keeping order, as you say, will keep you safe? Safety is an illusion. That house up there, it *is not* safe. You and that little girl *are not* safe."

I wish I weren't feeling so weak. I have the overwhelming urge to launch myself in front of Eva and stick up for Farrah. It's a strange urge, I know, but she's sick. She needs protecting.

Or maybe she doesn't.

Farrah stands, closing the space between Eva and herself.

"Hear this," the copper-haired girl says, peering down into the prophet's face in that stoic way of hers. So stoic it must be maddening. "You are not the first person ever to come to the Real Marvelous and spin wild tales. You are not even the first person to do so *this year*. Nor are you the only person claiming to have the ability to see the future and all the rot and death it holds." Farrah pauses to scan the bunkhouse. "You're right, though. My father and I are trying to maintain an illusion for my sister. We tell her every day that everything is going to be fine because that is what you do for children. You lie to them, so that they will feel safe in your certainty. Safety *is* an illusion, but there is safety *in* illusions, as well."

Farrah doesn't give Eva the opportunity to respond. She simply raises one eyebrow, backs away, steps from the bunkhouse and into the blistering heat of the late afternoon, and is gone.

THERE'S THIS TERM: *fever dream*. I've never understood what it really meant until now. In the past, my dreams were normal and coherent, boring really, when I'd compare them to other people's.

Now I have this surreal one—wild spun, as Farrah would say. I'm in a maguey field during a dust storm. I see a horse come charging down the row on a collision course with a man and a young boy. The horse is out of control, but I know I can stop it. I step in its path and somehow keep my balance in the wind. I wave my coa to try and distract it, but that doesn't work. The horse just rears up and cries out. I take the horse's reins in the attempt to steer it away, but the wind catches the animal, and it falls, crushing its rider under its weight. The horse then rights itself, and there, broken, dead in the dirt, is me. My eyes are wide but lifeless. My lips are frozen in a hideous death-smile. I'm covered in dust, already half buried.

Then the dream starts over.

NINETEEN

AGAIN AND AGAIN, Eva preaches. My fever days are filled with Eva's words, and there's nothing to do but listen to her praise the bees as if they were the gifts of an angry god.

They *meant* something, those bees, according to Eva. They were punishment. They were an omen of worse things to come.

You didn't think that was it, did you? Eva asks her followers, who huddle around her. *No, no. That was only the beginning. It will get much worse.*

My fever burns off in two or three or four days. I can't really tell, and it doesn't really matter. On the morning I emerge from the bunkhouse, I can tell camp has changed. It's all there in the weight of the air: there's a slow-burn anger, tucked away behind a thin veil of disappointment.

I've learned the names of some of the jimadors who died during the bee swarm. I recognize a few: Jenna, a girl who bunked next to me, and of course Raoul and Bruno. Leo is never found, and so his name is added to that list. Most names, though, belong to people I don't know or know only in passing.

I walk through a semi-empty camp, past the jimadors finishing their breakfast of powdered eggs and coffee. I see and hear things. Some say the fields will be shut down. Many have labeled the camp as cursed and have already fled for the trains. Rumors and conspiracies are whispered on the wind. The foremen are riding around looking for someone to step out of line so they can crack their whips. Their horses are hot and skittish. The kids in the mess crew, since they have fewer mouths to feed and clean up after, are playing this game that involves throwing kitchen knives at their own feet. Whoever gets closest wins.

I head up to the ranch house, passing first through the stables to check on King. Leo has been replaced by an older man named Ortiz who seems to know what he's doing. King is brushed and clean. The stables are tidy.

Ortiz says he heard about the brown horse, and I nod. He doesn't say "I'm sorry," which I appreciate. Then, without standing on ceremony, he tells me I'm wanted in the main house and turns to lead the way.

It's as I remember it: white, too white. Like last time, the windows are thrown open to allow the breezes to whip across the expansive tile floor. Ortiz tells me to wait in a large room off the entry and then disappears down one of the hallways.

I am, by far, the dirtiest thing in this house. I don't know how the floors and the furniture aren't coated with dust with the windows open like this. How are there no spiders or rows of ants crawling up the walls like in the bunkhouses? How is the floor so even? How does it smell like piñon pine and rosemary and not sweat and unwashed hair?

"Sarah Jac."

I spin around and see Bell standing in one of the hallways. She's wearing a dress. I've never seen her in a dress before. It's white and made of thin cotton fabric. Her feet are bare.

"Before she left, Farrah told me you were sick," she says.

Bell's feet are *bare*. I look down to my boots, once brown but now dishwater gray. They've been re-heeled at least three times. One has yellow laces; one has black. I've had them forever. Over the years, there have been scorpions in them. I've stepped on nails, glass, and cactus spines while wearing them. I've waded through questionable bodies of water in them, and they were once stolen from right off my feet while I was sleeping—this was in Chicago. When I found them abandoned in an alley, someone had used them as a toilet. I stood by while Lane bravely sprayed them down with a hose. Despite all that, they are my boots, and they protect me. They cover broken toenails and healed-over blisters. They give me the ability to *run*. Going barefoot is a luxury I could never afford. The last time my feet were clean and bare . . . I can't even remember. I was probably with James. He probably pulled my boots off himself. I close my eyes, shutting out the rest of that memory.

When I open them, there's still Bell and her bare feet, and that old anger swells.

"Before she left?" I ask, wondering if Farrah's visit *was* a scene from a fever dream.

Bell nods. "A couple of days ago she left to join Papá and James in El Paso. She's going to see a doctor there. To get better."

"Who will take care of you?"

"There are ladies here. They're nice. They help around the house."

"Show me your violin," I command.

BELL'S ROOM IS small and full of more white things: white curtains, white bedding, white-painted furniture, dolls wearing white dresses that don't look all that much unlike what Bell is wearing.

On top of her dresser is the violin.

"Have you been practicing?" I ask.

The little girl nods. "James helped a little."

"Can I see it?"

Bell picks up the violin and hands it over. It's wonderful. It looks even better in this bright room. There are a couple of minor nicks in the wood, but nothing that would affect the playability or the sound.

"I taught James his scales," I say, caressing the neck and running my fingers along the strings. There's a scab on my fingering hand, from where one of the many welts was. I must've picked it in my sleep.

"Can you play?" Bell asks. "Can you play something for me?"

"I can play." It feels strange to say this again. "It's been a while, though."

"Who taught you?"

"My mother."

"Play something," Bell urges, taking a seat on the edge of her bed. "Play your favorite song."

I think for a moment and can't help but grin. Maybe I *can* teach this little girl how to play and she'll learn how to put all the bad spirits to sleep, the ones that hover over the Real Marvelous. There's a song I used to play for Lane—a dumb little ditty, more fit for a fiddle than a proper violin. The words that went with it had something to do with a man whose car broke down, and in pushing it across the country, he'd picked up all these random hitchhikers: a nun, a former president, a teenage runaway. The song went on as long as Lane could come up with characters for it.

I bring the instrument to my shoulder and ready the bow.

I make the mistake, however, of looking at Bell on her bed with her clean, bare feet swinging off the edge. She pushes her copper hair away, revealing an expectant expression. A breeze enters through the window, catches all the white fabric, and sends it billowing. There's a view of the horse yard, but the blood is gone. I remember there being so much.

Bell got me once, asking me to show her how I could gallop. I may have pretended that triumph was mine, but she was the one who gave permission for it. She has some strange power over me. I won't let her get me again.

"I've forgotten," I say, giving the instrument back to Bell. She's disappointed, but that's fine. "It's been too long." I make a move for the door. "I need to get back to camp. I'm still not feeling well. I probably need to eat something."

That's not really true. I'm still a bit weak and queasy, but I've been faithfully taking the tincture Farrah brought me, and it has helped with the headaches.

Bell follows me out of her room and into the hallway. I hear her saying that there's plenty of food here in the house, but I ignore her.

"I'll tell Ortiz to have King ready tomorrow morning," I say over my shoulder as I bolt through the courtyard and back to the open space that feels like mine—even though nothing out here is really mine.

Bell doesn't follow me. She can't with her bare feet.

I thrust my hand into my pocket and finger her button charm. When I was sick in my cot and feeling unbalanced, the repetitive action calmed me down. I like the texture of it, that it's hard and solid and wrapped up tight.

But then I stop, and remember this: I don't believe in signs or symbols, but in reality, facts, and the things I can see with my own eyes. A freak storm of bees is just that: a freak storm of bees. It is not some kind of reckoning. An injured horse must be put down. Britain is not a stand-in for me. The Real Marvelous is not cursed; it is just a ranch full of sad people. Headaches are caused by stress and lack of water and malnutrition; they are not signs of all the bad to come. I am not being punished by unseen hands for the death of that foreman in Truth or Consequences. I just need to work. Work is all there is.

"I'll be back tomorrow morning," I say to Ortiz, who's in the process of loosening hay with a pitchfork. "You can have King ready then."

"I've been told Bell's not riding," he replies. "She's too upset. You're supposed to keep her company, though."

"What am I supposed to do with her?" I point to the house and raise my voice, half hoping Bell will hear. "I wasn't hired to be her playmate. I was hired to get her ready to be the replacement for her dying sister."

"You're just going to have to figure something else out," Ortiz says, his tone flat. He stops working, plunges his pitchfork into the hay, and leans against it. A scar runs down the length of his exposed forearm. "Given that you killed her horse."

Her horse.

"Tomorrow I'm going back to the fields," I say. "Come get me when Bell wants to ride again."

THE NEXT DAY, as I said I would, I go back out to cut maguey. I do the same thing the day after that and the day after that. No one comes to get me.

TWENTY

ONE NIGHT, AFTER James has been gone almost two weeks, I'm awoken by the sound of quick footsteps advancing in my direction. For a split second I think they belong to James, that he's come to wake me in secret, but then I realize they're too light to be his.

Someone crouches next to my bed. My body tenses.

"Sarah Jac!"

It's Odette. She places her hand on my shoulder, gives it a shake, and hisses my name again.

"There's something wrong with James!"

"What?" I whip around. "What is it?"

She doesn't say. Even though it's dark, I can see her trembling lip and the tears pooling in her eyes. Whatever she says will be terrible. She leans up against the frame of my bed, reaches for my hand, and threads her fingers with mine. At first I appreciate the intuitive, tender gesture, but then I remember that first day in the field, when she was trying to coax information from me about James' alleged girlfriend back in Chicago.

I relax, but just slightly. This is *her* ruse: play the innocent to get what she wants.

"Odette, what? Just tell me."

"He hasn't come back yet," she whispers, fighting back a sob. "He told me he would. Have *you* heard from him?"

She's trying to keep those big, round eyes shining innocently, but her mouth is set in a hard line, like she's expecting to be betrayed. Her grip is strong; her palm is slick with sweat. It's uncomfortable.

"No." I shake my head. "I haven't."

Odette closes her eyes and lets out a long exhale. "What is it, then? I don't understand. I mean, James was like your best friend, right?"

"Right," I mutter.

I want her to leave, but instead she just sits there, silent. I can feel her staring at me, waiting for me to tell her what to do. I, however, am not Eva. I don't predict the future. I don't need a follower, but I get the sense that Odette won't leave until I give her *something*. I refuse to say out loud that James might never return, so instead I say: "He'll come back. He's probably just busy working."

"Or," she says quietly, "he's under a spell."

"What?"

"He's under a spell," Odette repeats.

"Really, Odette. You can't be serious."

"Don't mock!" Odette glances around nervously. "It happens, Sarah Jac. I've seen it. We have no idea what Farrah's done to him."

"Odette, no. I've known James Holt for a very, very long time, and one thing I'm sure of is that he cannot be spellbound. It's not possible."

Odette is cringing, obviously not convinced, but eventually she nods her head. After giving her what I intend to be a reassuring squeeze, I withdraw my hand, and again wait for her to leave. Several seconds pass.

"Tell me a story," she says. "About James."

There are so many, and I don't want to give her any of them. I think for a moment, then choose one I can change. She'll believe the story is hers—or ours to share—but it will really still be mine.

"When we lived in Chicago," I begin, "James worked on train engines, and I was a waitress. One night, he stopped in after his shift and ordered a cup of coffee and a piece of blueberry pie. I looked at him like he'd lost it and told him that not a single blueberry—frozen or fresh—had graced this restaurant with its presence in all the time I'd worked there. Him asking for blueberry pie was like walking into a pet store and asking for a zebra."

Odette giggles. A berry of any kind is so rare it's practically legend. The weather is too extreme for anyone to grow them anymore. James, of course, knew that, too.

"He's always been optimistic like that," I tell her.

"Yeah." Odette lets out a sigh. "That's one of the reasons I love him so much."

There is more to the story, of course. I left out how that was the first night I met James. The diner had been empty until he came in, and when he'd rung the little bell on the counter, I'd been in the back, crying. Lane and I had walked out of the girls' home just a couple weeks earlier and were living on the street as thieves: always hungry, without home or direction. It was the most alone I'd ever felt.

At first I thought James was just plain dumb. But he wasn't dumb. He was optimistic. There's a difference. It was warm that day: the first warm day after a long, cold winter. James wanted blueberry pie so he asked for blueberry pie. He didn't care if some waitress gave him the side-eye because of it.

We had biscuits and little packets of grape jam, but for James, it was either blueberry pie or no pie. He ordered chili. When I set the bowl down in front of him, I pointed to his forehead and told him he had grease on his face. He grinned, leaned across the counter, swiped his dirty finger across my cheek, and called us even.

"I'm going back to sleep now," I tell Odette. "I'm sure we'll see James soon."

Still, Odette doesn't move, and because I once had a sister, I know exactly what she's doing.

I let out a long exhale. "Do you want to sleep here tonight?"

I scoot back to the far edge of my narrow bed and pat the

empty space on the mattress. Quickly, and without a word, Odette climbs up and nuzzles against me.

Again, I'm full of regret. We—James and I—shouldn't have chosen this love-starved girl. When we met her, that night she spoke of the bleeding maguey, she seemed so easy and innocent, but now she's morphed into something cagey and desperate, and, at times, scary like an injured animal. Or maybe she's always been this way. As I lie here, listening to her breathing even out toward sleep, I have to admit that I know very little about her other than the stories I've created.

THE NEXT MORNING, while I'm standing in the coa line, I watch a little boy pick a louse from his sister's head and then crush it between his fingernails. He finds another and does the same thing again. The next morning—a Sunday—I see three tiny, smashed bodies embedded in the coal soap of the bathhouse. That afternoon, the blankets are stripped from all the cots and put into vats of boiling vinegar. The women and men are separated, put in lines, and taken to our separate bathhouses. We're told to strip. Everything has to come off and go into a bucket. The girl in front of me must be about thirteen. She's sobbing as she takes off her clothes while at the same time tries to cover her developing body with her hands. Her modesty is almost touching. Who here is really modest anymore? When she hears the snip of scissors, she grips her long ash-blond hair in both her hands and starts to wail.

It's one woman's job to hack off as much hair as she can

with scissors, and it's another's job to wield a razor. Yet another woman has the unfortunate duty of inspecting our pubic hair for nits.

Once we're shorn of our hair, we're told to stand against the wall of the bathhouse and shut our eyes and mouths. We're hosed down with near-scalding water. Then we're told to wait for our clothes, which, when handed to us in a wad, are sopping wet and smell like vinegar. The thirteen-year-old girl holds her clothes bundle against her chest and shivers in place. Her face is streaked with tears, and she's gone quiet with humiliation.

I drag my wet clothes on as quickly as I can and step out into the sun to dry. The members of Eva's flock stand a few yards out, shoulder to shoulder, waiting silently with smug expressions for others to join them since the prophecy about the pestilence has been proven true.

"I told you!" Eva calls out. "It's the work of the witch!" Her eyes lock onto mine, and I wonder, for a moment, if she thinks it's me, if I'm the one who's caused all this.

Beyond Eva and her followers, beyond the ranch house, puffs of dust are rising over a hill. Another storm is coming.

Let it come.

Let it all come: the dust, the wind, the bees. I won't fight them anymore. I'm out of fight. My clothes are wet. I have no coa. I have no friends. I have no hair. I'm too thin. The wind could just pick me up and toss me into the sky, and I'd offer no resistance.

PART THREE

THE WITCH

TWENTY-ONE

I WAIT AND listen for the storm, but there's no hum, no whistle in the wind. Instead, there's something smoother, and stranger: the purr of a finely tuned motor. Other jimadors, freshly inspected, shorn, and washed, grow quiet and turn toward the sound. Mothers hush their children. We all watch as a long black car crests a hill and drives around the far end of the ranch house and out of sight. What I mistook for a storm is innocent dust kicked up by the car's tires. The driver announces his arrival with a toot of the horn, causing a woman next to me to gasp. Passenger cars—especially ones as sleek and pristine as this—are extraordinarily rare. Rare like a solitary deer glimpsed from a moving train.

I hear doors open and shut. Bell shouts out her sister's name. A diesel truck comes over the hill, followed by another one pulling a horse trailer. Men up there are talking. I pick out the words: *maguey, bees, lice, tired, agitación.* I trot forward, straining to pick out James' voice.

Odette follows me.

"He's back!" She grabs my arm, forcing me to halt. Like the rest of us, she's sunburned, bald, and pockmarked. Her eyes, however, are as clear and bright as pools people toss pennies into.

"He's back," I echo. I don't want to be swept up by a storm anymore.

This is what I hope will happen: James will come loping down the hill any moment now. Even though he'll see me right away, he'll greet the others before he greets me. There'll be handshakes and pats on backs. He'll hear about the bees and the people we've lost. His face will fall because he's tenderhearted. He'll let Odette fly into his arms and crush her in an embrace and tell her how much he missed her. After all that, he'll give me a hug, quick and firm, the type of hug you give your cousin. He may put his hand on the top of my freshly shaved head and laugh. It'll be unbearable, but I've come to expect nothing less.

This, though, is what actually happens: I wait for James as the sky darkens and the mess crew prepares the fire for supper. I stand in the mess line and stare down at my empty pewter plate, fighting the urge to look up at the house every other second. Warm light shines through the windows, and I wonder what the family is doing.

I pick at my soggy beans, unable to eat them because I'm so nervous.

I wait until the fires have died out, shivering against the cold.

I wait until everyone else has gone to the bunkhouses and the only camp sounds come from the wind and insects and dream-sighs of the jimadors. I'm awake in my bunk when the disappointment forms as a small burr nestled between my ribs. The deeper I inhale, the deeper that burr digs in.

I convince myself that James is still gone, and will never return.

THE NEXT MORNING, I head to the house. I can't avoid it any longer. Farrah must've seen me coming because she comes out to intercept me. The wind is a terror this morning, forcing me to keep hold of my hat and tossing Farrah's hair around wildly. She stops in front of me, and for a moment we're two wind-whipped girls staring at each other.

"I'm here for Bell," I say.

Farrah shakes her head. "She isn't well."

My eyes dart to the house. "What's wrong?"

"It's nothing. She's just in a mood. She'll get over it. Try back in a couple of days."

"I would think she'd be happy to have you back," I say.

"One would think that, yes."

Even after Farrah's gone back up the hill, I stay awhile, watching the house, wishing the wind would blow its walls down and reveal what's within. I want what's in there.

As I LIE in bed that night, the burr in my chest grows larger and sticks deeper. I get up a couple of times and walk around in the dark. I'm making up a conversation in my head with James, one in which I tell him how much I miss him, about how I'm ready *right this moment* to leave the desert forever and go to our house in the hill in the East. I tell him I'll be better, you know? Not so angry all the time. I'll find a book and read it or something. I'll make a friend.

The sun oozes red over the mountains the next morning, like blood welling from a long, shallow cut. I know this because I'm sitting cross-legged in the cold, watching it come up.

I've become a sitter and a waiter, sitting and waiting and willing. I'm no witch. If I am, I'm not a good one. I've cast out so many hopes into day and night skies, into fields, and out past mountains. I've cast them out like fluttering lures on long, long, nearly invisible fishing lines.

Witches can create things out of dust and air and intentions. They can cast out hopes and reel in something true. I can do none of this. I wish I could.

LATER THAT MORNING, when I see James in the fields, I almost drop my coa on my foot. I'm nearly sick with relief.

He's ridden out with Gonzales on a new horse—James' very own white horse, King's near twin. He and Gonzales stop in an open space about fifty yards away from me to consult with the overseer and a group of foremen. One of them sweeps out his arm, first in the direction of us jimadors, then out to an adjoining field containing several hectares of unharvested maguey plants.

That's when James turns and looks straight at me.

I lift my hand in greeting. He mirrors my gesture, but shifts his attention quickly away. A couple of moments later, Gonzales and his men start to ride out in the direction of the far fields, but James breaks off and heads toward me at a trot. I want to leap over maguey plants and run to meet him, but instead I slam my coa blade into the dirt to remind myself to stay in place. I bite the inside of my lower lip and try to hide a smile. As James approaches, I can tell he's doing the same thing. I can tell by the way he's forcing a frown.

When he gets close enough, I notice that he's clean in every way. His hair is cut and combed. His skin is smooth and paler, not like mine, which is tan and leathery from excessive sun. He's not wearing his sky-blue shirt but instead a white button-up and light brown pants so new they still have their creases. Those clothes fit like they were made for him. Not like his old shirt, which he bartered off some guy back in Tulsa.

He pulls the horse to a stop, dismounts, and then stands in front of me, surveying. I wonder if he disapproves of what he sees: a too-thin girl, her long dark hair gone. She's wearing old clothes that smell rank. Her skin is scabbed over and pebbled from bee stings. James' frown might not be forced after all.

I wait for him to say something, to tell me what the plan is, when we'll leave. I'm ready right now. I push the blade of my coa deeper into the earth. It makes me feel strong.

James smiles, just slightly, but it's enough. The scar on the side of his mouth tugs up. I resist the urge to reach out and touch it with my grimy finger, to dirty him up and bring him back to me.

He leans in. A light breeze comes through, carrying his scent to me. It's piñon pine and lavender. He's never smelled like this before.

"Your hair," he says in a voice that's just above a whisper.

A moment passes during which neither of us knows what to say. Actually, that's not true. There are thousands of things I want to say, but I don't want to say them here in the middle of this field.

"Nice horse." I extend my hand so the animal can get my scent. "What'd you have to do to get him?"

I'm joking, but James clucks and glances away. The horse, not interested, twitches and shirks from my touch.

"They're going to burn those maguey plants," James says. "The ones on the southern edge of the property."

"Why would they do that?"

"The bees. There were the workers that died on the day of the swarm of course, but there are also the ones that left after because they think this place is cursed. There aren't enough jimadors left to cut all that maguey before it rots. If we burn it now, we can at least replant for the next year."

"The jimadors that are left can work those fields," I say, corkscrewing my coa deeper into the earth. "We can get up earlier or work an hour later."

"Don't worry about the money, Sarah. I know that's what

you're doing in your head—counting up all the money you could make off that maguey."

That's not all I'm doing in my head.

"I've got you taken care of, alright? Remember that." James steps away and gets ready to mount his beautiful white horse. "I have to get back to Gonzales and the others. I'll find you later."

James rides away, but I remain still.

Odette's voice soars across the rows of plants.

"James!" she cries out, and then repeats his name at least three more times. He has to hear her, but he never even shifts in his saddle. Odette comes up and leans hard against me. She grips my hand, and I grip hers back.

I can't shake what James said, the way he said it: "*We* can at least replant for the next year." Followed by: "*I've* got *you* taken care of."

TWENTY-TWO

THERE'S A MEMORIAL service tonight. It wasn't planned, and it's not really organized. It starts at supper when one of the younger jimadors stands up to say something about his father, who died during the bee storm. Even though I can't understand all the Spanish he's speaking, I tear up as his voice breaks into sobs, and a woman—a sister, a wife—goes to him and gently leads him away. His is the first of many more improvised eulogies, all given in a jumble of languages and dialects. Jugs of pulque materialize and get passed around. Drinking triggers more speeches, longer speeches, speeches that detail happy and tragic childhoods spent in far-flung cities, formative years spent shivering on the streets in the rain or baking in trains, fortunes gloriously won and tragically lost.

There are lies told, I'm sure, and enhancements added, but all the tales end with this: a life cut short on a maguey field, a good person stuffed to bursting with bee venom or cut down in the ensuing chaos.

More mesquite logs are thrown onto the campfire. They burn fast and bright. I'm drunk and getting drunker and upset that no one's mentioned Raoul. I decide to speak on his behalf, even though I'm not really one for speaking. I stumble to my feet and deliver some words about a young man's honor and pride in his work. I don't mention how he died in the field, covered in dust, clutching the broken bundle of sticks that once hung around his throat.

"I watched him run!" I shout. "He ran until his legs gave out." The jimadors are gazing at me, some are weeping. "He may have fallen, but *we* were spared! This is a beautiful thing!"

Eva is silent at the back edge of the crowd, eyeing me uneasily. I decide it's best that I sit now. I realize, with a jolt, that I wish Leo was here. Or Bruno.

A couple of hours later, as the speeches taper off, the campfire dies down, and a deep cold settles into the desert, the workers start to retire to the bunkhouses. I'm not tired yet, so I sit next to a woman who lost her young son. It wasn't the bees that got him. He wasn't cut down by a blade, either. He'd actually made it to one of the trucks. He'd even helped her climb in behind him. On the way back to camp, the driver—maybe spooked by a bee that had flown into the cab—swerved sharply, causing the boy to fall from the bed of the truck. She tells me she can't stop hearing her son yelp—so small, she says, like a kitten—followed by the crack of his neck breaking.

I tell the woman I've lost someone, too. My sister. I tell her I held my sister's hand while she died.

I don't share these details of my life with many people, but here with this grieving woman, it feels okay to be vulnerable. We know sharp loss; we know each other.

The woman puts her rough hand on my cheek and shakes her head.

"Girl," she says in a pitying tone. "You don't understand. I lost my *child*."

I start to mutter a weak apology, but the woman cuts me off.

"It was no accident. The bees, their coming. My son, falling." The woman takes a swig from a flask and then glares into the glowing coals of the old fire. "You spend more time with that girl than the rest of us. You know what she can do."

It should come across as completely random: the association of Bell—*that girl*—with the deterioration of camp and the arrival of the bees, but in that drunken moment, it doesn't. It makes sense.

That girl. Not Farrah, as Odette thought. *Bell.*

"What do you know?" I ask.

"There are no accidents here," the woman repeats. "Years ago that girl was angry with her mother, something childish about not being given a horse of her own. The mother rode out, ignoring the fit her daughter was throwing, and almost instantly a clear day turned dark. Out in the distance, a wall of dust crashed down from the sky. We all watched from the fields as the woman's body was carried up, spinning." The old woman lifts her hand and twirls her index finger. "At first the wind was so strong, it ripped off bits of cloth from her dress, but then, all of a sudden, it stopped. The dust cloud disappeared. The woman hung there for a moment, suspended, her mouth open in shock. Then, she fell. For three days after, pieces of her torn dress were carried on the wind, drifting across the maguey."

This woman is not trying to convince me that her story is real. She is not gripping my hands in hers and pleading with her voice and her eyes. They all watched Bell's mother get swept up into the sky. Just like that. Simple. Bell and Bell's petty anger caused a freak windstorm. Not even a week ago, I would've scoffed at this woman and what I would've thought was her inability to grasp reality and responsibility.

But tonight. The stars in the night sky are overwhelming in number and in their random pattern. Some are glowing. Some are dim. Some are clustered, and others seem to stand apart. Someone has to be the first to point out how they connect. Constellations aren't obvious until the moment they are. Then you wonder how you hadn't been able to see them before when the pictures are all so clearly there, telling a story.

Bell was angry. Bell brought the wind that killed her mother. Bell was worried about her sister. Bell ruined the cornmeal. Bell made that mastiff attack Rosa. She brought the bees. Is this logic?

The woman hands over her flask. I tip my head back to take a drink, but keep my eyes closed so I can't see the stars. When I open them, I notice Odette, standing at the edge of a crowd of girls, staring at the ranch house.

I stand, wobbling. The old woman grasps my hand until I

find my balance. Suddenly, it is crucial that I get to Odette and tell her she was wrong. It's not Farrah casting spells. It's Bell.

I'm giddy with the news as I stumble over to her. She turns as she senses me coming. Her head tilts; her brows shove together. She's peering at me like I'm some curious creature. I realize I'm smiling. That must look so strange to her.

"Hey." I grab her wrist and pull her away from the others. "Remember what you were saying the other night . . ." I lower my voice. "About Farrah?"

Without all her waves of blond hair, Odette's large deer eyes appear even larger. She grips my hand, and again I'm startled by how strong this skin-and-bones girl is.

"What did she do?" she asks. "We should go up there, Sarah Jac. *Tonight.* I know which room is hers. I've seen her standing in her window before. I even know where we can get a knife. We have to find the evil and cut it out. We'll be heroes."

I balk. This isn't how I wanted this secret-sharing to go. How *did* I want it to go?

There's a buzzing in my ears. It sounds like the bee swarm, but I know it's from drinking too much. I sway a bit to one side, but Odette's iron grip holds me steady.

I can't possibly tell her about Bell. Bell is just a child. I can't bear the thought of Odette creeping into her room to carve her up with some rusty knife. Maybe she's not a witch. That old woman—maybe she was lying. Maybe she made it up. I wasn't there the day Bell's mother supposedly got swept up into the air. I didn't see it.

"What did Farrah do, Sarah Jac?" Odette urges.

I shake my head, but I can't for the life of me get my thoughts straight. I'm not thinking right. I'm thinking, *Protect Bell.*

"She killed her mother," I blurt. "That old lady over there told me. When she was a little girl, Farrah got mad at her mother for not letting her get her own horse so she cast a spell. The mother was tossed off her horse by a freak storm. They say Farrah caused it."

Odette releases my hand and takes a step back.

"But we can't go up there," I say. "No one would think we're heroes. They'd execute us."

"We have to save James," she whispers, placing her hand at her heart. "We have to get him out of there."

"We will. Just give me some time to make a plan."

I'M ON MY way to the bunkhouse when a figure emerges from the darkness between two buildings. My reaction time is slow. I stumble back just as a hand reaches out to catch me. It takes me a second to realize that the hand belongs to James. He's still wearing the clothes of an upper-class stranger, but the two top buttons of his shirt are undone, and I can see the sheen of sweat across his face and throat. Our hands clasp together, automatic, but his for some reason feels different. He leads me around the perimeter of camp to our spot behind the mess building, the same dark place where he first introduced me to Britain.

We haven't even reached a full stop before James brings his

mouth to mine. He's also been drinking. His lips are laced with the sweet smoke of tequila.

He pulls away too soon and studies me. His fingers dance gently across the fading welts on my face and collarbone. That's what's different: his hands. They're not rough anymore. The callouses are gone, sloughed off. His skin is soft; his touch, gentle—like he's sorry.

I don't want gentle. Or sorry. I press my mouth against his, desperately.

"You're different," I rasp. "More . . . put together."

James responds by grabbing a fistful of my shirt, pulling it up to expose my bare stomach. "Ruin me, then, Sarah. Pull me apart."

My hands grope at his face and his neck. What's happening isn't pretty, but it's what we both need. As always, we speak to each other best without words, through our bodies, the way they crash and intertwine.

Tonight our bodies say: *Thank you, thank you.* They say: *I thought you were gone, but now you're back.* They say: *I've missed your heat.* They say: *I want you. Just you. We will always be together. It must be this way.*

TWENTY-THREE

THE NEXT MORNING, as I'm waiting in the coa line and grinning to myself despite a raging pulque headache that even Farrah's medicine won't fix, Ortiz comes to tell me that Bell is ready to resume her lessons.

"So, she's better now?" I ask.

He shrugs. "I'll leave that for you to decide."

IN THE YARD, the two white horses are saddled and ready. Bell is there, but also Farrah, and they're both dressed in riding clothes. Bell is staring at the ground, sucking absently on a piece of hair. She couldn't be less of a threat. She's all innocence, not a witch of the wind. I'm disappointed in myself that I even entertained the thought.

Even mostly covered by her hat, Farrah's hair shines. James stands near the stables, talking to Ortiz and pretending like I'm not here. His hands are stuffed in the front pockets of a different—also new—pair of pants.

I miss those hands already, even if they're different now.

"Bell said she's enjoyed her time with you," Farrah says, tugging on her ivory-colored riding gloves and securing her hat. "I thought it might be nice if the three of us could go out together."

A command, not a suggestion. Farrah heads over to mount the new white horse and motions for Bell to go to King.

"We won't be gone long," she adds. "We're expected back in time for a late breakfast with our father."

I help Bell into the saddle and glance back at James. He's staring at me with eyes that are rimmed red from lack of sleep. He doesn't lift a hand to wave good-bye.

It's hot. Every morning is hot, but this one is particularly punishing. Farrah, naturally, seems unaffected. There are no little lines of sweat streaming down from where her head meets her hat. She's not wilting. She keeps her posture straight and her eyes focused on the mountainous horizon.

We ride in unsettling silence. There are questions I could ask: *How was your trip? How are you feeling?* Or things I could say: *Thank you for the medicine; it really helped. Odette—a girl you've never met—wants to kill you.* But I stay silent. Farrah might think I'm rude, or she might not think of me at all.

Our already short ride is cut even shorter because Bell starts complaining of a headache and claims she needs water. She's grumpy today, more so than usual. We're headed back to the house before we've even gone two miles.

"My sister tells me you know how to play the violin," Farrah eventually says.

"I used to. It's been a while."

"Was this back on the farm?"

"Yes." I pause. "My mother taught me the basics."

Something to the east catches Farrah's eye. "Look at that," she says, jutting her chin.

I swivel to the side, and sure enough, there in the distance, a tall, thin funnel shimmies across the plain. It's a dust devil. James once told me they form when hot air rises up quickly and smacks against a pocket of cold air. This is the desert. Hot air and cold air smack against each other all the time. So why does this far-off dust devil suddenly seem like some kind of omen?

"Bad luck," Bell mumbles, as if reading my thoughts.

Farrah ignores her sister. "So, anyway, Sarah Jac . . ." The horses pick up their pace. They see their yard up ahead and anticipate shade and water. "I just wanted to let you know that you're welcome to stay at the Real Marvelous as long as you see fit, and I hope we can become friends. You won't have to work in the fields anymore, and Papá has already started on the plans to build you your own comfortable outbuilding so that you can be in close proximity to us and the horses."

Farrah's talking in that particular way of hers again, using too many words, sounding too formal and neat.

"I'm sorry," I say, unable to hide my confusion. "I don't have to work?"

Farrah smiles, bigger this time, revealing a set of white,

straight teeth. I realize then that her eyes are also whiter, not so yellowed like they were before. Or maybe it's just a trick of the light. "James mentioned that you're very . . . oh, how did he put it? *Industrious.* He said you weren't really an idle person, which is why we thought you would enjoy continuing to help Ortiz with the horses. We're expecting a few more to arrive soon, and we'll need to expand the stables and practice yard. We just wouldn't want a member of James' family to be a common field hand. That was one of James' requests, and I agree completely."

I can see the yard up ahead and James standing at the gate, waiting for us to return. Farrah waves to him, but he doesn't wave back. His hands are still in his pockets.

"James is making requests?" I ask.

Farrah scans my face, her smile faltering. Doubt flickers in her now-healthy eyes. She recovers quickly, though, and snaps her smile back into place.

"Of course," she says cheerfully. "We'll talk more about it at breakfast. I'm sure you're hungry."

Farrah kicks her horse into a trot. Once she reaches the yard, she stops, dismounts, and hands the reins to Ortiz. She runs up to James, gives him a kiss on the cheek, and threads an arm through his. I watch them make their way toward the house, their steps matching in time, their heads bowed together.

Finally, James takes his left hand out from his pocket, and there, on his ring finger, is a metal band that gleams like fire in the morning sun.

I'M SEATED AT a long table in the Gonzales house.

There's talking and the clinking of silverware. Gonzales is there, at the head, and next to him is his overseer. Bell is to my left. Across from her is Farrah. Across from me is James, *my cousin*. In my mind, I'm circling him like a hawk. I hope he can feel my sharp gaze tearing deep gashes into his skin.

Everyone is eating. There are eggs and fried potatoes, rolls and fresh coffee. Bacon, even. My plate is full, but I'm just moving food around with my fork. I don't eat breakfast.

Bell is not happy. She's glaring at James, hawk-like, just like I am.

"She'll need a bit of time to get used to the idea of having new members of the family," Farrah says, reading her sister's expression. "It's been just the three of us for such a long time now."

Oh, but I don't want to be in this family. This family is nothing like me, and it's nothing like James. This family eats its breakfast off porcelain dishes using matching silver utensils in a house that's cool and breezy and smells of piñon pine. No one in this family is concerned with their body stink or parasites or if they're getting enough protein each day or with the fact that their shirt has a hole in the elbow that has needed patching for weeks.

Farrah is chattering on about how charming and kind James is and about the heartfelt vows he wrote himself and read aloud at the courthouse in El Paso just a handful of days ago. She fiddles with her ring, a simple silver band. She's so proud. She clasps on to James' arm and gifts him with a dazzling smile, bright like a diamond.

I catch Gonzales' gaze, and he raises an eyebrow. He knows things are being left unsaid, and it seems to trouble him. I can't imagine why he'd let a field hand marry his precious daughter, unless maybe he caught them in some kind of compromising position. My stomach lurches at the thought.

James is avoiding me. He takes a sip of coffee, as if everything at this family breakfast is just as it should be. That little sip is my breaking point.

"What is this?" I snap. "We never talked about this."

"Sarah Jac." James reaches over to give Farrah a reassuring squeeze on her knee. "I don't have to run every single detail of my life past you."

"Since when?"

James laughs, tensely, like he's embarrassed of me, like *I'm* the one making everyone uncomfortable here. "I realize this is sudden, but we'll have to talk later. Why don't you just eat some breakfast now, huh?"

I'm imagining creative ways to tear James to shreds as Bell quietly excuses herself to go to the bathroom. Gonzales launches into a gripe about how the mail seems to be getting more and more unreliable, and the worker standing behind him makes a promise to look into it. Another worker comes by and refills coffee from a silver urn. James thanks the man and stirs in two lumps of sugar.

Only now does he look up at me, holding my gaze as he takes another sip of coffee.

What are you doing? I ask silently. *What happened? Are you under a spell?*

But then, I wonder: Are we still working the ruse? Did James actually go so far as to marry a girl who is about to die in order to take over her fortune? Talk about hard hearts.

"Really Sarah, you should eat something," James says, lowering his cup to his saucer with a delicate clink. "I hear you haven't been feeling well."

I push my chair back from the table and mutter some excuse about forgetting something in the stables. Really I'm hoping to find some corner of the house and that James will follow me to it. I'm in the far hall when I hear the scraping of a chair. I cough, as a signal. Sure enough James finds me, like he always does. He takes my elbow and leads me around a corner, and then around another. We end up in a corridor near Bell's white bedroom. James spins me around to face him, and his expression is an unreadable knot.

"I can't believe you actually married her," I say. "So, what's the plan now?"

"There isn't any plan." James smells clean. I always want to be the one to touch him when he's clean. That scent, it dulls me a little, takes away my focus.

Ruin me, then, Sarah. Pull me apart.

"Listen to me," he commands, giving me a little shake. "This isn't part of any ruse. You can't be here anymore."

Silence hangs between us; from the other room, the silverware clinks.

"I don't get it," I finally say.

But, I *do* get it. I just don't want to admit it. I've lost James. I've always thought I would, but I never thought it would happen like this. I've always thought he'd start to feel like I was weighing him down—that I was a burden—and that he'd come to realize he'd be better off alone. I've never thought, though, that he would trade me for someone else.

I'm ashamed of myself for asking my next question because it's so sad, so last-ditch, but I ask it anyway. "Is this because I lost our money?"

"It's not . . ." James stops, frustrated. He takes a quick glance over his shoulder and then lowers his voice. "I can't explain this to you right now. You have to go."

"Go *where?*" My shame flips to anger. "Go East? Where there's water and boats and trees to climb? I gave Lane's necklace away so I could get you that pendant."

"You shouldn't have done that."

"How can you *possibly* do *this?*" I've spent most of this sorry excuse for a pleasant morning trying to keep my emotions tamped down, but now I can feel it—the pure, hot fury clawing its way up my throat, snaking its way down my limbs, and causing my hands to ball into fists. "She's *nothing* like us, James. She's not strong. Have you seen her hands? She's never worked."

"There are other ways to tell if a person is strong than by counting the callouses on their hands, Sarah."

I step back, stunned. The air leaves my lungs in one sharp, swift burst. I can't believe he just said that to me.

There's a noise in the hall, the squeak of shoes on tile. Far-rah calls out James' name. Her voice is rich and warm, like sunshine. I realize I haven't heard her cough once, not while we were riding, not during breakfast.

"She's not sick anymore," I whisper, the rage still crackling through my bones.

"Leave Valentine as soon as possible, tomorrow even." James starts to back away. "I'll find you later today. I'll give you some money, and then you go." James vanishes around a corner and into the clean hallways of his new home.

I stand there for a moment, telling myself that I'm strong and sharp, but it feels like I'm quaking, like I'm chipping apart.

Lane's necklace is gone. That last little bit of my sister. I can't believe James doesn't even care about Lane's necklace. It means nothing to him. He traded *us*. He traded me and Lane for Farrah and Bell. How could he do that?

This is not how this is supposed to work. *Leave before you're left*, my grandmother used to say.

Again, I wonder: Is this a spell, like Odette said? Is James under a spell?

I'm still standing there, trembling and alone in the hallway, when Bell has the bad luck of emerging from her room.

Bell, who just had pancakes with butter and agave nectar. Bell, who made her mother fly up to the sky only to bring her crashing down, who cursed the fields, who brought the bees, who brought the lice.

"You did this." I grab hold of the girl's arm and stare down into her wide eyes. "To James and Farrah. To James. You did something to him to make him fall in love with your sister."

Bell is silent, furrowing her little brow, pretending to be the innocent, as if she has no idea what I'm talking about.

"I know what you did to your mother," I growl.

"My mom?" Bell asks softly.

I lean in and tighten my grip. "You brought the wind." My fingers push easily into her soft muscle. She whimpers. "But I'm not afraid of you."

For a moment, Bell doesn't respond. Then she drops her gaze to her feet, which I take as an admission of guilt.

"I have something to show you." I pull Bell along behind me, and together we go out the front door, through the courtyard, and back in the direction of the horses. Bell skips and stumbles to keep up, but she doesn't make a sound. Of course she doesn't. She must be choking on her guilt. No one sees us.

King is tied up, but still saddled. As Bell and I pass the stables, I hear Ortiz inside, whistling to himself as he works.

"Where are we going?" Bell asks finally. She's tripping over her feet. Her hat's inside, so she shields her eyes against the sun with her hand and squints at me.

I know what I'm doing, but I don't. I untie King from his post, toss Bell up into the saddle, and climb up behind her.

"It's a surprise," I say, urging King into a canter and then quickly into a hard run.

Bell flops forward, then sideways, then has to catch her balance with the saddle horn. She clutches a handful of King's mane and yelps.

By now, the bellies of the Gonzales family are full. They've perhaps started to wonder what's keeping Bell and me. Ortiz may have heard the sound of King thundering away, but he also may have assumed that his new owner James Holt was taking him out. Once they all put the pieces together, Bell and I will be so far out that no one will be able to catch us with another horse. They'll send the trucks and cast a wide net, but I'll run zigzags to throw them off my trail.

My arms hurt from cutting maguey. My head hurts, and my skin still hurts from my fever. My lungs and my heart hurt. They feel heavy and full of salt. As I ride, the pain finds a rhythm. It's not soothing exactly, but there's something nice about a rhythm even if there's pain involved.

Bell may be saying things—shouting even—from her position in front of me, but I'm so focused I don't hear her.

We've gone a few miles before I pull King to a stop. I've been crisscrossing the plain and can tell by the sun that I'm facing west and by the shadows that it's almost noon. A bird cries out. Aside from that, it's so quiet my ears buzz.

This is as good a place as any.

I dismount and drag a crying Bell from the horse. Her legs have gone limp. She falls to the ground and makes no attempt to get up. She covers her face with her hands, and I can see the sunburn on them.

"Take off your boots," I demand.

"I'm thirsty," she whimpers.

"Take them off!"

Bell doesn't move, so I kneel down and yank her boots off myself. Her cries ratchet up into wails, but beyond those, I can hear something else: a train whistle in the distance, coming in from the north by the sound of it.

"Stop being a baby," I say.

The little girl hiccups and wipes the snot from her face. "What are you doing?"

"It's a game." I stand and stuff Bell's boots into King's saddlebag. "If your sister loves you enough, she'll come find you."

I mount King, and Bell pushes up to unsteady feet. Her socks are gleaming white. Her cheeks are streaked red from the sun and from crying. She's a tiny thing, pitiful in the purest sense.

"I don't want to play a game!"

Bell lunges toward the horse and grabs for the stirrups, but I jerk King away and scan the horizon for the clouds of dust kicked up by car tires or the bold glare of a white horse. They'll probably be on their way by now.

"Sarah Jac, please!"

Ignoring Bell's cries, I urge King into a hard gallop in the direction of what I hope are the train tracks.

TWENTY-FOUR

I HAVEN'T GONE far, probably not even a mile, before I spot a cluster of black birds, three or four of them, soaring lazily past me in the direction of the ranch and of Bell, who's dissolved into just a speck in the desert now.

So small. Bell will die, from exposure and dehydration, probably in a matter of hours. That's what I wanted. But now the thought of Bell lying there, peering up to the sky, watching the great black birds she's so fond of expectantly circle her body, suddenly makes me sick. I realize now—late, too late—that I don't want anyone to die. I just want the Gonzales family—and James, oh God James—to hurt, to hurt like I've been hurt.

I stop King, turn him hard, and take off again. When she finally comes into view, my eyes skip over Bell at first. How quickly she's started to disappear into the landscape and become a tiny pile in the dirt, barely noticeable except for her white socks. She's sitting down, still crying.

I jump down from King and start to search the ground.

"Your sock!" I demand. "Give me your sock."

I find a stick, a sturdy one, almost a yard long, and drive it into the ground. Bell's doing nothing but staring and hiccupping, so I strip off one of her socks myself, tear its edge, and then drive it down onto the tip of the stick. There's just enough wind to catch the sock, but not enough to blow the whole thing over. It's not a perfect flag, but it'll do.

"Don't move!" I tell Bell as I remount King. "Don't try to walk home. Just wait until your sister comes."

"Stay with me," she begs.

I can't stay with her. After what I've done, I'll be dragged back to camp, shot, and probably fed to the remaining mastiff.

Just as I'm urging King away again, I hear the sound of a rifle shot. King startles, and as I work to steady him, I scan the desert. My heavy, salt-filled heart lurches in my chest. I take a breath in, and am surprised by how loud it is. There's another shot: a crack and then its echo.

If it's James, I can outride him. Maybe. I dig my heels into King's side, and push him into another hard gallop. I can tell he's tiring. I wish I were on Britain. For me, she would have run and run and run.

I look over my shoulder, see the other white horse in the distance, and that James is, in fact, its rider. The gun goes off again—the shot's not directed at me, but skyward. King whinnies and twists; the reins whip out of my hands, and I nearly fall from the saddle in the attempt to get them back. James fires another shot, and King is done. He stops and rears back on his hind legs. I'm thrown forward, clinging to his mane to keep my balance.

King lands hard on his front hooves, shakes his head, and is still. I can hear everything: my deep breaths, King's deep breaths, the buzz of an empty landscape, the whistle of the still-distant train, and the pounding of the other horse's hooves.

I pitch forward in the saddle and roar with frustration. The wind blows crosswise, spraying dirt and small rocks across my face, like it's chastising me, like it's saying, *You idiot girl. Look what you've done.*

"Please, King," I beg. "I need you to run. I need you to get me out of here."

King must be feeling generous. When I dig in with my heels, he snorts and breaks into a run, but it's too late. James is coming in fast at a diagonal and soon enough lines his horse up next to mine. For a moment, we're matched, galloping stride for stride, heartbeat for heartbeat.

"Stop!" James shouts.

I try to pull away, but James reaches out and yanks at my reins. King, unsure of what to do, veers right, straight into the other horse. As they collide, James leans over, throws his arm around my midsection, and manages to drag me off my saddle and onto the front of his. I let out a humiliated, strangled cry. I kick my legs, but they find nothing except air. It's no use. I'm stomach-side down. My view is of saddle leather and, if I rotate my head, a tilted, bobbing horizon. I try to go limp, so that I'll slide off and fall hard to the ground, but James has one hand on the waist of my pants to hold me in place.

"Where?" James shouts.

I point weakly in the direction of where I left Bell, and James steers his horse that way.

It only takes a few minutes for James to locate Bell, still sitting next to the makeshift white flag, and when we reach her, James flies off his horse and runs to scoop her up. I slide off the saddle and stand aside. I lost my hat, so I keep putting my hand on the top of my head, as if that makes any difference.

I can see a burn on the exposed part of Bell's neck that has started to blister. Her lips are cracking. James grabs a canteen from his saddlebag and urges her to drink. When she's had her fill, he takes his own pull, and then holds the canteen out to me.

I shake my head.

"Fuck you, Sarah." He walks over and shoves the canteen into my chest. "Drink some fucking water."

I take a small sip—any more than that and I'd throw up.

"Your horse isn't going to make it," James says.

I glance back and see King coming toward us at a trot. Why he followed us I have no idea.

"I'm not going to run him anymore."

I return the canteen and watch James try to get Bell to drink a little more. She won't. The water just spills down her chin and onto the front of her shirt.

James takes one last pull and wipes his mouth with his sleeve.

"What were you thinking?" he snarls. "You could've done whatever you wanted to me—I expected that—but I *never* would've expected you to take this out on a little girl." For a brief moment, he peers out to the mountains; then his eyes land back on mine. "Gonzales will kill you, you know. Then he'll string up your corpse at camp for everyone to see."

I say nothing as James hoists Bell up under his arm and mounts his horse one-handed.

"You tried to run away," he says. "Like a coward."

He's right.

We walk the horses so we don't wear them out. I'm back on King. About a mile out from the house, James stops so he can bind my hands with rope and lead King by his reins. He needs to make it appear like I'm his prisoner. After losing our bearings several times, having to retrace our steps and double back, it's midafternoon before the house is in sight. I see Farrah first. She's standing at the edge of the horse yard. She lets out a shout when she sees her sister sitting in the saddle in front of James and runs up to meet them.

I'm watching Gonzales watch me. His face is tight with rage, which I expected. I've taken one of his fragile treasures and nearly crushed it.

Once Bell is safe in her father's arms and the horses are tied up, James drags me down from my horse and sets me on legs that sting from dehydration.

He isn't able to free my hands from their bindings before

Farrah approaches and slaps me across the face. I'm surprised by her strength.

"Bitch," she growls.

I take that insult, fold it up, and keep it safe with all the others.

TWENTY-FIVE

MY GRANDMOTHER USED to say that the best thing to be is useful. She said that if you had a group of twenty people, only two or three of them would be of any use. The rest of them would lack common sense and what she called *intestinal fortitude*. A useful person can, among other things, start a fire, hunt small game with a rifle, witch water, tell time by the position of the sun, determine whether or not a plant is poisonous, and soothe a crying baby.

Above all, a useful person knows her place. She doesn't draw attention to herself and does what needs to be done, nothing more.

My grandmother would not be very proud of me right now.

AFTER FARRAH HIT me, Gonzales locked me up. He had Ortiz lead me through the camp, where the jimadors were just returning from the fields, to a small room in the back of a storage building.

"You made a mistake, girl," Ortiz said. I can't help but hear an echo of what Leo told me that night in the stables, when he said James was in the house *with* Farrah.

In the room, there's a cot with a straw mattress and a metal folding chair. There's one window, a small one, roughly the size of a shoe box, up by the ceiling. The walls are made from vertical planks of wood, crudely and halfheartedly hammered together. I could break out of this room if I wanted with a well-placed kick, but I won't.

I've been here for two days. The gaps in the boards let in the cold air at night, and, during the day, lines of sunshine stretch across the dirt floor. I can hear everything: people walking around, of course, but also Eva's now-nightly sermons about judgment and punishment, faraway train whistles, men taking a piss onto a nearby scrub oak, and animals—javelina hogs most likely—snorting and shuffling after nightfall as they search for trash.

Aside from the sounds, there are the smells that make up the overwhelming rot-stench of camp. It reeks of carcass and horse shit, especially in the hot afternoons when the mess crew is starting to cook what passes for food these days. I can't believe I've stayed at the Real Marvelous this long—in this filth. I've become the filth.

There's a padlock on the other side of the door. I told Ortiz before he left that he didn't have to lock me in, just like James didn't have to bind my hands when he led me back from the plain. I'm not going anywhere. Ortiz bolted the door anyway. *Just to be safe*, he said.

I've had no visitors except for Ortiz. He's been designated my warden. He brings food, and we sometimes play cards together. He's made distinctive nicks in the corners of all fifty-two of the cards so he can tell what he's dealt and what he's drawn. He always wins.

Ortiz remains tight-lipped. I thought that maybe since he keeps winning hand after hand he might reward me with news about how Bell is faring or if Gonzales has said anything about my fate. I make jokes about Eva: *What a piece of work, huh?* I tease him about what it's like to be my servant: *I bet the horses smell better than me, right?* I ask him if he's ever seen an execution at camp before: *How many? Did Gonzales make everyone watch? Did the people up there waiting to be shot start to wail or did they stay silent like Bruno did?*

He answers only the last question, about the executions. "I've seen a couple. Maybe three. But once, some kid who stabbed a foreman in the leg begged for forgiveness in front of Gonzales and the whole camp and was spared. So there's that."

So there's that.

Ortiz comes in one morning and hands me a letter, written in pencil on a yellowed page torn from a book. It's from Odette. Her handwriting looks like mine: terrible, all gapped and slanted.

Don't worry, it says. *I'm going to help you.*

Later that night, James comes. I hear someone working the lock and assume it's Ortiz. I'm half asleep, so I call out something about how he can wait until the morning to fleece me at cards again, but when I turn my head and see a familiar profile in the doorway, I sit up suddenly and reach for a sun hat Ortiz lent me and place it on top of my fuzzy head. After all that's happened, I'm still trying to impress him. *Still.* Because he's James, and he's beautiful, and we once made plans together.

James enters and closes the door behind him. He's in a new set of clean clothes and is wearing camel-brown boots that are shiny and just barely covered with dust. He doesn't ask how I'm doing. I don't expect him to. I'm tired and angry. I have so many questions, but James doesn't give me the chance to fire off even one.

"I'm not going to fix your mistakes anymore, Sarah." He reaches into his back pocket and pulls out an envelope. "This is the last time."

"That's what you think you've been doing? Fixing my mistakes?"

"Yes."

"You think I've been the weak link?"

James steps forward, lifting the envelope so that it's hovering right in front of my nose. I slap it away.

"Just because I'm not leaving doesn't mean you can't." He shoves the envelope into my stomach the way he did with the canteen a few days ago.

I take it, warily, and peek inside. It's stuffed with more paper bills than I've ever seen. It makes me think of the money I've got hidden in my bandanna. The money I earned working day after day in the fields and with Bell doesn't come anywhere close to the amount in this envelope.

"What is this?" I ask.

James takes a breath. "I promised."

Then it clicks, what he said the other day: *I've got* you *taken care of.*

I hurl the envelope at James, wishing it were a brick. It hits him in the chest, and the bills scatter to the ground. He doesn't even blink.

"Have you spent so much time up at the house in bed with *your girl* that you don't see what's happening here?" I seethe. "We're starving. People are losing their minds. Bruno. I got caught in a bee swarm, and my horse . . ." I trail off. "I could've left weeks ago—hopped one of those trains just like everyone else with sense. Left with the caravan. Instead I waited here . . . with you. *For* you."

James crosses his arms over his chest and looks to the ground. It's the first time I've seen him appear even remotely guilty.

"What about the other night?" My voice breaks. "When you came back, and you found me. James. You're *married*?"

"Sarah . . . I already told you . . ."

I rise from the cot and start pacing. "How did this even happen? How did you . . . ?"

James reaches out to stop me, but I spin from his grasp.

"Don't touch me." I point my dirty finger into his clean face. "You do not get to touch me *ever* again."

I rake my fingernails across my shorn head and, in the process, knock my hat off. James bends to pick it up and then places it on the edge of my cot. It's a gentle, considerate gesture.

His hand—the left one—lingers on my hat, as if that will have to do since I won't let him touch me. There's no gold band around the third finger. My gaze travels to his collar. There's no pin, no gift from another desperate girl.

Hope flares. It is so small, though. And undeserved.

"Come with me," I beg. "Just come."

James lets go of my hat and puts his left hand back in his pocket.

"I can't."

A sob rises in my throat, so big I nearly choke on it. "I thought she was dying."

It's a terrible, illogical thing to say, as if love and death are mutually exclusive. James knows this, and doesn't dignify it with a response.

"This . . . This isn't you. This is James playing dress-up."

"Just take the money and go."

"You're hiding behind fancy boots and a new haircut."

"Sarah." There's a roughness to the way James says my name, like he's coming apart inside, the way a pile of rocks shudders before collapsing under its own weight.

Come apart, I urge silently.

"Does your Farrah know you're a gambler and a thief and a killer?"

I'm trying to threaten him, but he doesn't take the bait. "She knows more than you think she knows."

"Did you tell her about Tulsa? About Truth or Consequences? Does her father know?"

James is silent, and that is my answer. Gonzales knows. Farrah knows. With James connected to the family, they would have protected me, but now I either die here or get hauled back to New Mexico and die there.

"Take the money and leave, Sarah Jac," James says. "No one knows I brought it."

Die here or die there. Either way, I'm old bones in the desert. I take a step toward him, crunching paper money under my boots. He smells the way he always smells now, like piñon pine. And faintly of dust.

"No."

"We can stage it," James says. There he is, my schemer. "We can make it look like you attacked me. Beat me senseless. Use your fists. Use that chair over there. Knock me out, take the money, and go."

"Tell me what happened with Farrah," I demand.

"I fell in love with her, and I married her."

"Liar," I scoff.

"I told you I didn't want to do this forever, Sarah—hop trains with you, be on the run all the time."

"We had a plan! Did you not think about me at all?"

"A *plan*?" James extends his arm, gesturing to the fields and bunkhouses beyond the wall. "Have you seen these people here? You don't think they all had plans when they were our age? We could work for decades running little scams and cutting maguey, but it wouldn't amount to anything."

"What does that mean?" I demand. "*Amount to anything?* I had no idea you cared so much about nice clothes and fancy cars."

"It's not that!" James moves past me, brushing up against my shoulder, and sits on the side of my cot. He runs his hands through his hair, loosening it from its pomade. A lock comes free and hangs in a crescent at his forehead.

"Of course I thought about you," he says, "and in thinking about you I figured out a way to help you *and* myself, and you went and fucked it up!" He pauses, and I watch him breathe heavily, as if he's exhausted, as if I've exhausted him. "I'm sorry about what happened to you, Sarah—the bees, Britain. I wish I could have been there for you."

I wait for him to say he's sorry about Lane's necklace. Or that he's sorry for marrying Farrah. Or that he still loves me. Seconds pass, maybe a full minute. He says none of those things, so I give up and play the only hand I have left.

"I look forward to dying here," I declare, proud of how steady and clean my voice sounds.

James lifts his head, and his eyes widen.

"Burned at the stake like a witch. Or shot in front of everyone. And I look forward to what's left of me being strung up on a pole in the center of camp. That way you can see me every day from the window of your beautiful new home and watch the vultures come to slowly pick my carcass apart."

James flinches, just slightly, then rises to stand. He regards me for a moment, quietly.

"Hard hearts, James Holt," I say.

"Suit yourself," he replies, moving past me to get to the door. "I have to go. No one knows I'm here."

"How's Bell?" I call out as James places his hand on the door latch.

He stops and glances over his shoulder. "Don't act like you care, Sarah Jac."

After James leaves and I'm again alone in the locked room, I kneel down and carefully collect all the paper money that's scattered across the floor. The bills are mixed. Some are ones; those are crumpled and worn. Others are fives. Far more are twenties, crisp and bank-fresh. I take my time sorting them on the mattress. I count them once, then twice, then a third time just to be sure. I put them back into their envelope and shove the envelope into my waistband.

For a long time, my little room sings with James' presence.

TWENTY-SIX

I'VE STOPPED PLAYING cards with Ortiz. I don't trust myself with my bets now that I have all this money from James.

Odette finally comes. Early one morning before the trucks leave, I wake to the sound of her whispering my name through a gap in the wall.

"Sarah Jac, it's me! Did you get my letter?"

I roll from my cot and move across the small room toward the sound of her voice. She reaches her dust-covered fingers through the gap to awkwardly clasp on to mine.

"Has James come to see you?" she asks.

"Yes," I reply. "But just once. And not for long."

"Not me." Odette sounds like she's choking: on her sadness, on her anger. "I bet he wants to come, but that bitch won't let him."

She gasps and releases my hand. She stands; her boots shuffle. Her bandaged foot is right in front of me. The cloth wrappings are clean, coated in dirt rather than blood. I wonder how much it still hurts her. I know she still limps.

"I'll come back," Odette whispers. Then she's gone.

Later, in the afternoon, I'm dozing when I again hear my name, again called through the cracks. It's brighter now, so when I flip onto my side, I see a brown eye peering at me. It blinks. Several sets of dirty little fingers poke through the gaps. I rise, and the eye and fingers vanish. There are multiple squeals, followed by the sound of several sets of feet running. I've become something out of a storybook, a girl-monster that the kids of the Real Marvelous can't resist waking only to run away from.

I kill time envisioning a new house—not the one in the hill, but one out here in the desert. Of course it'll be smaller than the Gonzales estate, where James and Farrah will tumble around together under cool white sheets, but the sandy color will be the same, and I'll figure out how to set up the windows and doors so that the breezes come in but the dust stays outside. I try to imagine myself living there with Bruno, but all I can recall anymore is his warmth, the script of his tattoo, and the smell of his cigarettes. I can't picture his face. I know we talked to each other several times, but all I can hear in my head is him asking, *Did I do the right thing, Sarah?* And then, in the fields, him telling me to *go*. I can't make a full person out of just those scraps, so I imagine living in my house alone.

I'm thinking about my desert house when James comes back. He looks more like how James should look—dirtier, rougher around the edges. He's wearing the same pants and shirt as the last time I saw him—the shirt for sure. It's wrinkled as if it's been slept in for several nights. He's rolled up the sleeves to his elbows, like he does when he goes to work in the fields, and his cuffs are smudged with dirt. His ring is back on.

I sit up.

"Odette's trying to find—"

He cuts me off, shaking his head in warning. Then, Bell enters.

Her hands and face are smeared with some kind of white salve that I'm guessing is meant to soothe her sunburn. Aside from that she seems well enough. I remember thinking she looked full of cake when I first saw her standing in the horse yard, and full of cake she looks again. The desert didn't do its duty with her. It didn't dry her out and cripple her. Bell's cheeks are still plump, and she's standing straight and proud. I know her well enough to see she's angry.

"She followed me," James says.

"You had a sister," Bell blurts out. "She died. James told me."

I glare at James. As if he hadn't betrayed me enough.

"How old was she?" Bell asks.

I clear my throat. "She was a little older than you."

"Do you miss her?"

"Yes. Every day."

"I could've been your new little sister," Bell says.

The right thing for me to do would be to apologize. I'd take Bell's small, warm hand in mine and tell her I wasn't thinking straight when I rode her out on King and abandoned her to the elements. I would say that there are things in my life that are really complicated right now and that I hope she'll forgive me one day, though I'll understand if she won't.

Instead, I say: "I don't want a new little sister. And if I did, you, Bell, could never replace the one I had."

"Sarah," James warns.

Bell's eyes pool with tears, but still she's undeterred. "I asked Leo one time why you were so mean, and he said that you were lonely. He was trying to be your friend, but you wouldn't let him."

"James, what is this?" I ask. "Am I supposed to explain all this to her? Do *you* want to?"

"Bell." James puts his hand on the little girl's shoulder. It's then I notice the third finger on his right hand; the entire thing is swollen, purple to nearly black in places. Bell shrugs James' hand away. She doesn't want his comfort.

"Just say what you came to say and let's go," James urges.

Bell says nothing, and I assume she's waiting for me to do or say something. She's wearing her riding boots, the ones I shoved in King's saddlebag. They've gotten dusty from the trek across camp.

"James says you're going away," Bell finally says, "so I just wanted to say thank you for the riding lessons. I learned a lot, and I'll miss you."

This little girl—what is she doing to me? She's thanking me? She'll *miss* me? Does she not understand what I tried to do to her? Does she not understand . . . *anything* that is happening here? I reach into my pocket. Bell's button is still there, wrapped in wire.

"James," I say. "Can you give us a minute, please?"

"I don't think so." James reaches for the little girl's hand, and again Bell dodges away from him.

"It's okay." I force a weak smile. "She'll be fine. I promise."

James is reluctant, of course, but Bell doesn't seem at all afraid of me. A single tear, large and shiny, rolls down her chubby cheek, and she wipes it away roughly as if she's ashamed of it.

"Ten minutes," I say.

"Five," James counters. "I'll be right outside. Just call out if you need me, Bell."

I wait until James has gone and then reach out to take gentle hold of Bell's arm, which is slick from lotion.

"You don't like him," I say. "James."

Bell shakes her head and looks over her shoulder to make sure that James is gone.

"I don't like him being around my sister all the time. I wish he'd go away."

I study her for a moment. For such a young girl, she's so fearful, so angry. What does she do with all that anger and fear? Where does it go when she's so stuffed and can't hold it all in?

"I need to ask you something," I say. "And I need for you to be as honest as possible, okay?"

Bell nods. "Okay."

"Do you . . . ?" I trail off in an attempt to find the way to make what I'm about to say sound less bizarre. "Have you ever made . . . things happen? I mean, have you ever been mad or sad or scared and then noticed that something strange happened?"

"What do you mean *something strange?*" Bell asks.

"Well." I pause. "Maybe the weather changed suddenly? Or maybe the animals acted differently, or maybe even *people* acted differently? Like, all of a sudden someone you thought you knew seemed like a stranger, or all of a sudden they're hurt or sick? Has anything like that ever happened?"

Bell doesn't speak, but she tilts her head and bites her lip. Lane used to do this when she was embarrassed.

"It's okay," I say. "I won't tell anyone."

Another tear slips down Bell's cheek. "I'm sorry."

I move off the bed and kneel down in front of her. "You don't have to be sorry. But it's happened?"

Bell nods. "After my mom died, I couldn't stop crying. Papá told me I cried for three whole days, and then on the fourth day, the rains came. It hadn't rained for years, he said, and it rained and rained and ruined all the plants and one of the horses drowned. He told me that it was all my fault and that I was bad luck. Then he said that if I hadn't been acting like such a baby, my mom would have been more careful while she was riding. He said she'd still be alive if it wasn't for me. He told me I'm probably the reason Farrah's sick now." Bell gasps, hiccups. Her words have all come out so fast. "He says I'm a witch."

I sit back on my heels and sigh. Now I see: Bell's father is full of magical thinking, too. A wife dead, crops ruined, and a daughter sick have become so much, so unbearable that he blames it all on his littlest offspring.

"You are not a witch," I say.

"I am!" she exclaims, sniffling. "You said so, too. I put a curse on James. I put a charm under his cot in the stables. I used one of my teeth that had fallen out and wrapped it up in black cloth and yarn like my mother taught me. Then I burned it in the dirt. It's supposed to make him sick, and I think it's working. Did you see his hand?"

"Why would you try to curse James?"

Bell lowers her gaze and shakes her head. "I don't want my sister to love him."

"Why not?"

"Because then he'll take her away and leave me here alone." Bell comes closer. Her hair is downy soft against my cheek, as she whispers in my ear: "I hate this place, Sarah Jac. I wish it would all blow away."

The door opens, and James reenters. He stands—how he's always stood—rooted slightly heavier in his left foot than his right, causing his left shoulder to pop forward. It's so slight. By a glance you'd think he was perfectly symmetrical.

Farrah can't possibly see this. There's no way she can see him with the same amount of detail I do.

"You told Bell I'm going away?" I ask. "When is that supposed to happen?"

"Bell," James says, "wait outside, please."

I release the little girl, sit back on my cot, and watch as she walks away. She waves. It's a tiny, forlorn gesture. I wave back, and Bell closes the door behind her. It's probably the last time I'll ever see her.

"Tomorrow," James says. "Just before supper. Gonzales will do it himself. In front of everyone."

"You'll be there?"

"Of course." James pulls one of his hands out of his pocket and checks his watch—the first I've ever seen him wear. "What did you do with the money I gave you?"

"Nothing. What would I have done with it, bought myself a new car?"

"An eastbound train comes in forty minutes," James says. "If you go now you can catch it. Transfer south and cross the Mexican border. I sent word to Leo to be on the lookout for you."

I blink, reach out and grab James by the wrist as he's turning to go. I can feel his pulse in my fingers, erratic and racing. "What about Leo?"

He glances at my hand. "I thought you knew."

"No. Farrah told me he . . ." I hunt for the right word. ". . . vanished. She assumed he'd died when the bees came."

"He went south to Ojinaga the morning before the bees. He'd saved up enough to buy some land. It's not the greatest. It's full of half-burned and rotted-out maguey, but he's already planted his first crop. You can work for him." James pauses. "I thought you knew all this. He sent me a cable while I was in El Paso. I wrote you a letter."

That morning at the breakfast—the one where the path of

my life swerved hard and I became a villain—Gonzales was complaining about the mail. Would a letter from James, about Leo and the possibility of a different future, have made all the difference? I don't think so. I never would've left the Real Marvelous without James.

I swallow. "Does he know about Raoul?"

"I told him."

"He never said he was leaving."

James shrugs. I watch his eyes travel from the shadow of hair on my head to the bee-sting scars on my cheek and jaw to the stubborn yellowish bruise under my eye from where I hit my face on the dashboard. His eyes travel down, to the hand that still holds his wrist, and to the discoloration on my skin from welts that never healed right.

"What happened to that finger?" I ask. "It looks like you crushed it in a door."

"Spider bite. At least I think so. I woke up and it was like this. I can't think what else it would be. Hurts like crazy, though."

"You need to lance it."

"I will."

"What about Chicago?" I clear my throat. "I need to get back. For Lane."

"I think you should let that go, Sarah."

For a moment, we're together, close but not close. I figure it's the last time I'll ever get to touch him, so I give it another shot: "I'll go, but only if you come with me."

James shakes his head and gently pulls his hand away. "You can still make it if you run," he says. "Just go, Sarah."

Bruno said *go*. James says *go*.

I stay.

THAT NIGHT I can't keep thoughts about my life—not my house in the hill or in the desert, but my *real* life—out of my head. It starts with the farm and my grandmother telling me how desperate people were when she was a little girl. They'd come down from Chicago, most of them on foot, begging for food or a place to stay. She was young then, but she remembered her grandfather sitting on the porch all hours of the day with his shotgun across his knees, telling these tired and hungry people to move on.

"I didn't understand then," she told me. "I thought he was just being cruel. I learned later that desperate people turn, like an apple gone to rot from the inside out. Most of them can't be trusted. The ones that *can* be trusted will most likely figure things out on their own."

I remember my grandmother teaching Lane and me how to take care of ourselves and each other. We learned to bake bread from yeast we caught in the windowsill and set traps and tend to the livestock, but most of all we learned how to work hard without complaining.

I remember one time when I was ten and got cocky when I was learning to ride. A horse bucked me, and I fell and dislocated my right shoulder. I was either too afraid or too proud to tell my grandmother, so I just sat in that field until nightfall. When she found me, she shoved a hunk of leather in my mouth, told me to bite down, and jammed my shoulder back into place. It healed, but it never healed right.

There was the time when Lane and I were out gathering berries, and I looked up to see a child I didn't know trying to talk Lane into coming with her to play in the road. The next thing I know, my grandmother comes tearing from the house with her shotgun and aims those two barrels straight at that child's forehead. Lane started crying, and I nearly did, too. My grandmother told us to get in the house. I never did hear a shot.

My mother. She played the violin and taught me enough about music so that I could teach myself the rest. What I remember most about her was that she had blond hair the color of Lane's and that she gazed out the front windows of the farmhouse and cried a lot. I don't even really remember her face because it was always angled toward that window. Then one day she was just gone. She left in the night without saying goodbye to any of us. I've never missed her, and throughout my life never wished she was around to comfort me when times got tough. She needed to comfort herself most of all—that's what *she* needed. Maybe that finally happened. I don't know.

My most crystal memories are from that farmhouse. My memories from Chicago come in small snatches. There was the feel of my sister's hand when we were marched into the boardinghouse. It was small and cold, her skin shriveled like a piece of paper that had been wadded into a ball and then smoothed back out. The springs on my bunk at the boardinghouse were so old and tired they made a noise if I exhaled too loudly. On the wall next to my pillow were scratches made by the fingernails of the girl who bunked there before me, who learned her ABCs but never quite got to proper reading and writing. There were just random letters strung together. Sometimes there was a word, like *were* or *salt*, but I think those were accidents.

We were not beaten at the boardinghouse. We were not underfed, and no one was particularly cruel to us, except for those times when the housemother would catch Lane trying to kiss the other girls. Then the nuns would beat Lane's butt with a paddle in front of everyone. Lane would stare me down, silently begging me to save her, but I never did. Later I told her that if she was that determined, she needed to learn how to get better at sneaking around.

The reason we left the boardinghouse was simple: Lane and I were used to a certain kind of freedom and were determined to have it again. And we did, at least for a little while.

We had a room in a walk-up by the water. It was the room that Lane died in. Our downstairs neighbors ate a lot of cabbage, and our room constantly stank of it. My sister and I would climb the fire escape to watch sunsets on the roof. The air wasn't exactly what you would call fresh, but at least it didn't smell like cabbage. There were no stars to see in Chicago, but we remembered the constellations we learned at the farm—Virgo, the Dippers—and would point to the sky as if those constellations were still there. We'd make up new ones and give them names like the Butcher of South America and the Mighty Kitten. We'd even sit up there in the dead of winter. We'd screech and hunch together, refusing to be defeated by the cold wind. I remember Lane's arms: tiny, flimsy things.

On one of the tables in the diner where I first met James, there was a brown ring left by a coffee cup. It never came clean no matter how hard I scrubbed it.

I don't remember the first time James kissed me, but I do remember the second. We'd spent too much money to see a movie that wasn't any good. We were walking home when he pulled me into an alley and pressed me gently against the side of a brick building. There wasn't any privacy—people were everywhere, trains always tore through—but James had the ability to make the big world seem small. He brushed my hair away from my face. I hooked my pointer finger into his belt loop and tugged. We fit so perfectly together.

I remember Lane's dead body and how, after a couple of days, her jaw started hinging open to reveal a tongue turned green-gray. It was time then, when she started to look like she was silently moaning, to let her go—even though I fought against it.

There is so much wind in the world. I learned that on the trains. The wind made me happy again. That and space and

James' good nature. We'd jump trains when we needed money. Even in our most desperate times, James would say or do something that would make me laugh, like when he ordered blueberry pie or came up with the most daring plans.

I'd forgotten about that, all the laughing.

I haven't had the worst life.

TWENTY-SEVEN

ON THE DAY I die, I get to take a shower.

But before I'm escorted to the bathhouse, I take my bandanna out from the waist of my jeans and stuff it and its contents in the envelope James gave me. I give that envelope to Ortiz and ask him to hide it in the stables until he can find a way to send it to Leo Sanchez in Ojinaga, Chihuahua, Mexico. I ask him to send it anonymously, but Leo will figure out who it's from if he remembers my bandanna.

It's a present forged from guilt, but it's a present all the same. I looked to Leo and saw an enemy. I did that out of habit. If Bell was right, he was trying to be my friend, but it had been so long since somebody tried to be my friend, I couldn't put the pieces together.

"Can I trust you to send it?" I ask Ortiz.

He thinks a moment before he replies. "I'll send it. I promise. It's bad luck to lie to a person who's about to die."

• • •

THE WATER IN the shower isn't very warm, but I stay in for a long time anyway. I scrub my skin with coal soap until it's pink. I pick out the dirt from underneath my fingernails and try not to notice the short lifeline on my palm. My feet, though, they're beyond saving. They could belong to a mummy. A horse once stamped on one of my pinkie toes, and ever since then the nail refused to grow. Both my big toes are cocked inward, and the nails are yellow and thick.

When I emerge scrubbed clean, the sun is still high in the sky. The air smells strange, different from the usual scent of human and animal filth. It's acrid, sweet, and smoky. Like diesel, but not quite. I realize it must be all the burned and burning maguey, all those plants that couldn't be harvested, all that money wasted.

The jimadors are gathered around the center of camp, which means that work was cut short today so that I could have an audience. The overseer binds my hands behind my back, grabs me by the upper arm, and marches me through the crowd. His mastiff shuffles and grunts along beside him. The jimadors are quiet, but the kids are babbling at one another or squatting and drawing circles in the dirt with their fingers.

I scan the crowd for familiar faces: Eva, Odette (who never did come back to visit me like she said she would), Ortiz, even the ghost of Bruno, who either had a lovely heart that was destroyed by the desert or a brutal nature that the desert revealed. I will miss them, all of them. But it's too bright for me to see at a distance. I wasn't allowed to wear my sun hat.

A ten-foot wood pole stands, upright, a few yards beyond where the campfire has just been started in preparation for supper. I have a vision of myself, tied up and shrieking, as I'm burned at the stake. It will be slow and painful, and I'll have to watch everyone watching me die.

This scares the living shit out of me.

But then I see Gonzales, standing off to the right, holding a double-barrel shotgun down by his side. James is there, too. He's next to Farrah. Her copper hair is flying westward. James has a fresh set of clothes on. His hair is combed back. I'd like to think he got clean just for me. As I pass him, I see he's wearing his old boots again, the ones he's had forever, the ones that have taken him across rivers and state lines. He has on mirrored sunglasses, so I can't see his eyes. Bell is not there, thank God.

I'm made to stand against the pole and face the jimadors while Gonzales steps forward to tell the crowd why they're all gathered.

"This girl is a liar and a criminal," he says, which is undeniably true. "She put herself into my good graces only to abandon my youngest daughter to the elements and leave her for dead."

Gonzales pauses, as if waiting for a response from the crowd. Nothing comes.

He goes on to tell them that I will be put to death here as a reminder that the Real Marvelous does not tolerate insubordination or harbor criminals, and that no traitorous deed will go unpunished. The crowd, to their credit, remains silent. Over their heads, the mountains in the distance are coffee-colored and dotted with dark green.

Apparently, I'll get no opportunity to plead my case or give any last words, which is fine. I deserve this fate: for Bell, for Angus. The overseer works to fasten my blindfold, and I'm sad that the last thing I'll smell is some sweat-soaked rag. The last thing I'll see, as the overseer makes adjustments to the blindfold, is a nearby jimador flinch and slap his arm.

For a moment, I hear nothing of note, only the sound of someone coughing and my own breath as I'm trying my best to smooth it out. Why I still find the need to impress these people with my stoicism, I have no idea. James has always said that I was strong. I should be proving him wrong. I should be gasping for air, pissing myself, visibly shaking with fear, and shrieking a newfound allegiance to the gods above.

I'm no saint. I shouldn't be trying to act like one.

Gonzales' boots crunch against the dirt, but at the same time I hear something else. It's a hum that comes from the east, a hum that starts off in dissonant strains but then melds together like an orchestra tuning. The jimadors start to chatter. There's the sound of wind, arriving in a great, sudden gust.

Someone screams, and I'm sprayed with dust. A rifle goes off, and my legs give out. I stumble back against the pole, and the back of my head knocks against the wood. My ears ring. It takes me a second to realize I'm not dead. I heard the shot, which means I'm not dead. I'm hit again with blowing rocks and dust. But when the rocks cling and start to probe my skin, I realize they're not rocks. They're bees. They're crawling on my arms and my face, in my hair. The mastiff—I can hear it bark and then yelp, the pitch so high it hurts my ears.

I fall to my knees, collapse to my side, and attempt to writhe against the ground to push off my blindfold. Pain shoots up my spine in two places. I scream, my teeth scraping against the dirt.

I'm thinking that I'll die here pathetically, blind and tied, when I'm hauled up to unsteady feet. My blindfold is stripped off, and I blink. The sunlight is patchy, streaming weakly through hovering black clouds of bees. I'm stung on the neck and the wrist and try to twist away from the pain.

"Hold still!" I hear Gonzales shout.

He slams me back against the post, steps away, and loads two fresh shells into the rifle. A bee skips across his eyebrow. I might have died there, on the ground from stings, but Gonzales wants my death for himself. It doesn't even seem to matter that the Real Marvelous is in the process of coming undone around him.

He takes aim. My eyes are open, staring into twin black barrels, so close I can smell the powder burn from the last shot. Gonzales cocks the hammer back. My stomach clenches with the click.

Something zips into my field of vision from the side, skimming just past the tip of my nose. I think for a second that it's a bee, but it can't be. It's too big. There's a flash, clean and bright, followed by a crack so loud I scream. I feel a sizzle against my cheek and again, thinking I'm shot, I lose the strength in my legs.

Someone catches me. The tension on my bound hands increases for a second, then releases. I'm free, and someone has hold of one of my wrists. It's James. In his other hand is Gonzales' rifle. He flips it around and plows the butt end into Gonzales' forehead. The owner crumples to the ground. James then crouches down, snatches his bone-handled knife from the dirt, and slides it back into his boot.

James threw his knife: to hit the gun, to hit Gonzales. I don't have time to ask what he's done or why he's done it because he's pulling me away from the center of camp and toward the diesel trucks, which are all parked in a row at the far edge of camp.

James' sunglasses are gone, and a couple of bees are on his face, tiptoeing over the sweat near his brow and the bridge of his nose. Another dances across his collar. He doesn't even try to swat them away.

I run, but I'm breathless and can't get into a stride. My skin is on fire. I'm stumbling, seeing double.

Behind me, from the center of camp, a too-familiar voice cries out and brings me to a halt.

"Burn them!"

I yank my arm from James' grip and spin around. There's Eva, running barefoot past the campfire, holding a makeshift bramble torch above her head. The flame appears to ripple slowly, like a bright orange flag catching the slightest breeze.

This is her time—to bring forth the destruction of everything she believes is meant to destroy us. It's the rebirth she's been talking about. Fire is the ultimate cleanser. Fire will scorch the earth, and new, pure things will emerge from it.

Her eyes are wide, lit with satisfaction. Like the bees have come at her request and fire burns because she asks it to. Like *she* is the witch she's been warning about. The jimadors are hers to control—this she believes. If she lives through this day, what a tale Eva will have to tell of her triumph.

"Burn it all down!" she shouts.

And they do. The jimadors snatch up logs from the fire and swipe them through the air to fend off the bees. But their aim isn't true. They're spinning in circles, setting other people's—or their own—clothes on fire, setting the bunkhouse walls on fire.

Others run up the hill toward the ranch house. Foremen on horseback attempt to cut them off. They're smashing jimadors' faces with rifle butts. Some are fast and are getting through, though. I could get through, I bet. A part of me wishes I were with them, rushing to that house, screaming at the top of my lungs. There are things I want in there: eggshells, a violin, Bell.

Bell. Where is Bell? Where is Farrah, and why is she not with James?

A new wave of jimadors advance toward the house. These have coas in their hands. The supply shed's been raided. There are bodies on the ground around it, bodies that are twitching and oozing blood that quickly turns black in the heat. The foremen guarding the ranch house flip their guns and start firing. Inside the house, glass breaks; a window explodes. Soon, the house will burn, too.

I watch as Bell and Farrah emerge from around the back. In the chaos, Farrah went to the house for her sister. That's what I would have done, too: found Lane first. Farrah's tugging Bell along behind her, urging her short legs to pump faster. The sisters are skirting the far edge of camp, in the direction of the stables, where the horses are and where all my money is stuffed in an envelope.

My money.

I sprint away from James and hear him behind me, shouting. He's trying to grab me, pull me back.

"We need to leave!" His desperate fingers brushing against mine. "Sarah, no!"

Up ahead, windows are shattering from inside the house and the back edge of the building has started to smoke. Still, I keep running because without the money, where will I go? James was right about that. I'll go to another maguey field and work for next to nothing. I can drive one of the trucks until the tank runs out of gas, but that could be a matter of hours. Maybe less. Then what? I walk? Not likely. Not for long.

I reach the stables. The thick smoke inside is keeping most of the bees away, but a few still hover lazily.

A woman rushes past me, carrying a bundle in her arm, a baby. In her other hand is a pitchfork. This is what she thinks she needs right now. This is how her brain is working.

"Ortiz!" I cry out.

I don't wait for a response before I run over to his cot and flip it over. James has come up beside me and together we search through a pile of old magazines and scattered playing cards until we find my envelope. I snatch it and straighten up, covering my mouth and nose with the sleeve of my shirt to shield myself from the smoke.

I turn to the doorway and stop. Farrah's there, gripping Leo's old shotgun. Her copper hair is undone, puffed as if she's been swatting at it. Her dark pants are coated in dust, and her sweat-soaked shirt clings to her skin; it's the most savage I've ever seen her. The hand not holding the shotgun is gripping Bell by the shoulder, keeping her steady. The little girl seems to see me but not really. She mumbles my name, her head lolling.

"Did you do this, Bell?" I run toward her. "Did you bring the bees?"

The little girl is too out of it to answer. I look to Farrah and see her eyes locked on a spot behind me, where James is standing. I know the expression in her eyes: betrayal laced with confusion. I saw it in Odette, on the night of the traveling show, when she watched James lean in and say something that made Farrah light up with laughter. I saw it in Lane, when the head-mistress at the girls' home was whipping her butt with a paddle and I just stood by. I saw it in Raoul, in the stables, when I walked in on him and Leo. And I saw it in Bell, when I left her in the desert to die.

She wants to know, but is too proud to ask, why, when all hell was breaking loose, did James help me and not her?

James offers no explanation. There isn't time for one anyway. He darts in the direction of the horses. He opens their pens and smacks their sides to get them moving.

"Let's go," James commands. "Everyone. Now."

"Her foot," Farrah says, motioning to Bell.

I look down and see that Bell's foot is a mangled mess, crushed and bleeding, as if it's been trampled. James scoops her up with one hand and throws her over his shoulder. He leans in to Farrah and says something I can't hear. Farrah doesn't respond; she pretends he's not even there.

"Go!" James shouts. "To the trucks."

We follow his command and run. Outside, the noise is awful: the low symphonic hum of the bees, the screaming of horses and humans, the screeches and pops of fire.

Camp burns. The buildings are on fire. People are on fire. Bodies—puffed from stings or slashed by coas—litter the ground. The white horses thunder past me, on their way to run wild in the desert. *Where will they go? How long will they last?*

James races past me, a limp Bell still slung over his shoulder. Most of the trucks are already gone, and another is in the process of pulling away.

I've lost sight of Farrah, so I look over my shoulder. She's several yards back, doubled over and gasping for breath.

"Farrah, run!" I shout.

She ignores me, and instead straightens up to better scan the camp. She must be searching for her father. He might be on one of the trucks already, but with his bad leg it's more likely he didn't make it.

I watch as bees land on Farrah's face and the exposed skin of her arms. She shrieks, stumbles forward a few feet, drops her rifle, and falls to the ground.

"Get up!" I cry out.

"Sarah!" James shouts from up ahead. "Sarah, move!"

I stop, bracing my hands on my knees, and try to catch my breath. I can see James at the truck, placing Bell in the cab and then working to hot-wire the engine. A group of jimadors advances toward him. They're covered in blood. They're holding coas covered in blood. James sees them and stops working for just as long as it takes to get his knife out from his boot and clamp it between his teeth. Then he shifts his focus back on the engine.

At the back of the pack of advancing jimadors is Odette. She notices Farrah, stalled and helpless, and breaks off in her direction. A couple of bees wander across Odette's nearly bare skull, but her attention is fixed. She's gripping the handle of a coa just as she would to strike maguey. She's limping because of her bad foot.

"Farrah!" I shout, bolting in her direction.

Farrah turns and sees Odette. She digs her fingers into the dirt, clutching the earth as if it will keep her steady.

I hear the truck roar to life behind me.

I'm fast, but Odette had too much of a lead on me. She advances, lifting her coa, readying for a strike that she knows will land true. Her face is . . . *radiant*, lit with pride and happiness. She is finally doing something. She is *finally* making things right.

I'm closer now, just a few yards away. Farrah cranes her neck to look up at Odette. Her hair, even now, glitters in the sun. She blinks at the crescent of metal that hovers over her face. She says nothing, doesn't even open her mouth. Her head shifts to the side a little; her brows crease, as if she's silently asking a question. Without answering that question and without mercy, Odette drives the blade into Farrah's neck.

I watch it all: Farrah, lifting her hand to her throat, as if she could knit the skin there back together; Odette, raising the coa again; Farrah, collapsing, her blood soaking into the strands of her hair. I scream. Over the sound of my scream comes the blare of a horn. I turn my head, and there, almost a hundred yards out, is the truck, headed toward the horizon without me.

I feel a warm, slick hand grasp mine. It belongs to Odette. I know that without even having to look. She tightens her grip and tries to pull me with her back to camp, as if that's where she and I and all the other cursed souls belong. I don't want to look down at Farrah again, but I can hear her: gurgling, gasping, her legs kicking helplessly against the dirt. I smell the fresh blood, earthy and bright, and I gag.

"I'm sorry," I say. "We never meant for this to happen."

Odette tilts her head and gazes at me, confused. Her

expression is just like Farrah's was when she saw the coa blade raised above her head. I pull my hand away and take off in the direction of the truck.

James isn't slowing for me. I dodge the other jimadors and then break into open ground. When I've made up half the distance, I see James lean across the cab and throw open the passenger door. I push harder, get as close as I can, and lunge forward. My fingers miss the door by inches, and I crash to the ground, landing on my knees in a creosote bush. I spit into the dirt and squint up toward the truck. James still hasn't slowed. He knows how fast I can run and that I can make it.

I haul myself up and take off again, my right knee bursting with pain. The passenger door is still open. I hear the rush of blood behind my ears, a rush of wind, and the sound of my boots hitting the ground. It's just like being on a horse. Britain. My Britain.

Something in my brain switches, and I feel no pain. I reach the open door, get a solid hold on the frame with both my hands, and launch myself into the cab. I slam the door shut behind me, and the cab is quiet. The engine is loud, yes, but at least the screams from camp are drowned out.

I straighten up in the seat and notice Bell flopped against James, her eyes barely open. She's been stung, but not too many times from what I can see. I'm dizzy. I lean forward and put my head between my knees. I can still smell the blood—Farrah's blood—on my shirt. It's sticky between my fingers. I'm certain I'll throw up, but after a few moments, the nausea passes.

I sit back and look to James. There's a large welt underneath his ear. His face is flushed, and he's sweating like he's fevered.

"She brought the bees," I gasp. "She wanted the Real Marvelous to disappear. She told me. She put a curse on you. Your finger."

James says nothing. He just stares straight ahead. I can see the tight cords of muscle in his neck. He's hurting, and I'm not sure I can ever fix him.

"I'm sorry," I say. "I tried."

That's not good enough, and we know it. We killed Farrah, the both of us, together. James shakes his head, just slightly, indicating that he doesn't want to talk about it.

TWENTY-EIGHT

IT'S EASY TO lie.

Like this: My name is Sofia Hale. My husband's name is John. We have an adopted, copper-haired daughter named Frances. We're from Chicago, where John worked as a mechanic in the rail yards and I worked as a waitress until we'd saved enough money to move south and buy this cheap parcel of land. We live in a modest ranch house we call the Lone Crow in the northern Mexican state of Chihuahua.

That last part isn't a lie. Neither is all this: We bought the land we live on from our friend Leo Sanchez and hope to expand upon it soon. Our principal crop is maguey, which, after harvesting, we send off to be distilled into mescal.

We've heard from others about what happened up north, at the Real Marvelous, about how, after suffering one too many indignities, the jimadors staged an uprising. They set fire to the crops and killed the men in charge. They burned the camp to the ground. Whoever was left after that, fled—disappeared like dust. The land is empty, but no one wants it now. People say it's cursed.

We do not kid ourselves in the desert: life is hard here, even in the best of circumstances. We still work all day in the sun, harvesting our own crops.

JAMES AND I sleep in the same bed at night. We have for a long time. It's only when we're lying side by side together under layers of wool blankets that I call him James and he calls me Sarah. Our real names have become our gifts to each other. When James says my name, he runs his hands through my chestnut brown hair—I've come to like it shaggy and short—and he studies me with his moss-green eyes. Sometimes he says my full name, Sarah Jacqueline, and drags it out long. But he doesn't do that as much as he used to.

"Are you happy?" he asks.

"Yes," I reply. This is sometimes a lie, sometimes not. It's hard to be happy when guilt and memories come and crush me with a force that nearly cracks my spine. But sometimes we lie for the people we love.

Also, sometimes James thinks things he doesn't say. I can tell when he does this. He didn't do it before he took the job at the house at the Real Marvelous. I've accepted it, but I don't like it. A part of him has been chipped off and is lost to me. Maybe not forever. I hope not forever.

I believe that James really did love Farrah. I want to think that's because he's always loved people with imperfections, people that my grandmother used to refer to as *crooked timber*, but I don't know if it's fair to describe Farrah this way.

James didn't save Farrah, though. He saved me. This means something.

Only once did I ask him why he chose me, and he didn't answer.

James tells me he loves me, and I wonder if the spell he was under is wearing off. He says it when he runs his hands through my hair at night and calls me Sarah. But there's something between us, like we haven't forgiven each other completely. I sometimes catch James staring at me, like he's just remembering I'm here. His hands still don't always feel like his hands, even with fresh callouses. This worries me. But we've started to laugh again.

He has this scar on the side of his mouth. When he smiles it tugs up, like a needle pulling thread through fabric.

I believe him when he tells me he thought he was doing the right thing by marrying Farrah, the right thing for both of us. He was wrong, but he thought he was right.

Late one night, as we're sitting around a campfire with Leo, James tells me something I'd suspected when we were at the Real Marvelous. Farrah knew about Truth or Consequences. James let her in on this secret the night before they were married in El Paso. Farrah never held it over our heads, James said, but still he had to think of a way to protect me. He had to come up with a plan.

"You should never have made a plan without me," I said. "That never works. We have to do things together."

"We have to do things together," he echoed.

Leo had been looking off into the dark distance, but he turned his head, and his eyes locked onto mine. They shone in the firelight. I knew he was going to tell me something about lies and liars, and how they're both inescapable because they're part of the fabric of this earth. Lies built empires here and have destroyed things much bigger than the Real Marvelous.

Instead, he smiled and said, "I'm glad you finally made it here, Sarah Jac."

JAMES AND I have never gone back to Chicago to get Lane her proper grave marker, and I've let go of that plan. But there's a canyon out here, a big, deep one with the thinnest trickling river at the bottom. I've named it Lane, which was actually James' idea, and sometimes I go and sit on the edge and tell Lane about my life. Or I lie on my back and watch the stars with Lane right there next to me. I've always had these little things of hers, a lock of hair or a necklace, but now I've given her something ancient and big, and that's better, I think.

BELL AND I still go out riding together. She's now on her own horse. I've taught her how to tell time from the angle of shadows and how to use a knife to shave the spines off a nopal cactus so that she can eat one if she ever finds herself lost or her canteen runs out of water. At the house, I've shown her how to catch yeast in a clean jar and eventually make bread from it.

She's a quick learner, and I'm proud of her. Sometimes,

though, she has nightmares. She wakes up screaming, but can never remember what it was she was dreaming about. She doesn't say much about her sister, but maybe she will as time goes on. Or maybe she won't. I won't press her on it. I know it's good to have secrets about a sister, so that she'll live brightly in the heart and no one else will ever be able to claim her.

Bell likes it when James tells her stories, the ones he says aren't true but really are, the ones about two orphan girls who run away from a boardinghouse and have adventures in a big city. She will, at random times, smell smoke when there's nothing on fire. She claims, on some mornings, that the birds are talking to her, trying to give her a message. I've caught her before, standing outside as the sun rises, whispering to the wind. And just once, as she was doing this, I watched as a dust devil whipped by.

By mistake, we have made a family, and I hope it won't break. I hope I don't break it.

After Bell and I go out riding, I usually drop her off at the house and take off by myself. My new horse is a red roan. I haven't given her a name yet. She's strong and fast. We go far together. I often wonder, when we're tearing across the desert, what would happen if we just kept going, if I never turned her back. Would she take me all the way to the ocean?

THE END

ACKNOWLEDGMENTS

Please allow me to thank . . .

My teachers; my students; my family; my friends, particularly the hags in the bog, particularly Stephanie Kuehn, for reading an early version of this novel and giving it its name, and Kate Hart, for reading an early version of this novel and demanding, *More Eva*; April Genevieve Tucholke, for her humbling words that grace the back of the book; all the readers, teachers, librarians, and writers I've met in my travels, for their kindness, their support, and for allowing me to bend their ears; my dream team at Algonquin Young Readers, including Krestyna Lypen, Elise Howard, Eileen Lawrence, Trevor Ingerson, Jacquelynn Burke, and one of the earliest true fans of this novel, Sarah Alpert; my agent, Claire Anderson-Wheeler at Regal Hoffman, for loving this novel in the blink of an eye; Michelle Andelman, for loving it first; the town and people of Marfa, Texas; and, lastly, my dear Jeff, who loves the West more than anyone I know.

There are many works of art that influenced *All the Wind in the World*, and I'd like to mention some of them here, including the novels *Gold Fame Citrus* by Claire Vaye Watkins; *Station Eleven* by Emily St. John Mandel; *Ship Breaker* by Paolo Bacigalupi; and *The Road* by Cormac McCarthy. The character of Sarah Jacqueline was inspired in part by the character of Mia in Andrea Arnold's film *Fish Tank*, and there is no way my novel would exist without the extraordinary influence of Terrence Malick's film *Days of Heaven*. Thank you to these artists for their art.

Get swept away by another forbidden
romance in Samantha Mabry's
A Fierce and Subtle Poison

I MET MARISOL on a Sunday night, two days before her body washed up on Condado Beach. We were sitting across from one another in a field near El Morro drinking rum from a bottle I'd lifted from the hotel. She was one of Ruben's cousins, and he was there, too, along with Rico, Carlos, and some girls they all knew from school.

This is how things typically went: A girl would come over and run her fingertips across the back of my hand or the top of my knee. She'd look at me, her eyelids heavy, and say something about how her older brother or her uncle would kill me if they knew that she was hanging out with me. She'd mention my blond hair, my dad, and how she and the other locals didn't know whether or not he was saving their island or ruining it. She'd give me some version of some lesson she learned from her cousin in New York or Chicago or wherever about how white guys really know what it meant to treat a girl the way she deserves to be treated.

Eventually, I'd take her by the hand and lead her either into one of the narrow alleys between the Spanish-style buildings or down to the footpaths outside of El Morro near the ancient mangrove trees that reminded me of the gray ghosts of giants. In the attempt to convince her that I was cultured and interesting, I'd tell this girl about all the places I'd traveled and sights I'd seen. I'd tuck the stray hairs that fell in her face behind her ear. I'd be gentle, my touch featherlight. I'd look her in the eye and ask permission to kiss her.

She'd always say yes.

Marisol was different, though. She didn't mention anything about my blond hair or developer dad. She did come and sit by me, but after telling me her name, she said she remembered me from last summer, when she and Ruth—a giggling girl who was currently pawing at Rico—saw me at a party. She asked if I remembered her. I told her I did even though I didn't. Which was a shame. I should've. Marisol had a generous, loud laugh, a distinctive heart-shaped face, and straight, waist-length coffee-colored hair, the shade of which almost exactly matched her eyes.

She shifted onto her knees and nervously plucked at a blade of grass.

"I was hoping you'd come back," she said.

My head was already swirling from the rum, and I was only half listening. The way Marisol was sitting caused her butter-yellow dress to ride up high on her thighs. I wanted to reach out and touch the place where hem met skin.

"Let's take a walk," I suggested.

We snuck away and stumbled down a steep path that would lead us closer to the water. We faced a murky expanse of sea. Behind us was a section of the original walls of the city, built hundreds of years ago to protect San Juan from invaders. Forty feet up and on the other side of that wall was the dark and silent courtyard belonging to the house at the end of Calle Sol.

This spot was a favorite of mine, quiet and isolated. I could stand there for hours and wonder if I had the nerve to jump into that inky water and start swimming. When my arms got tired, I'd float. I sometimes couldn't imagine anything better than being alone in the ocean, carried along by the currents, with my arms out wide and the light from the moon and the sun bathing my face.

I never told any of the girls about my dreams of floating in the ocean. I also never mentioned how I always wondered if the wish on a scrap of paper I'd tossed into that nearby courtyard five summers ago was still up there, waiting to be granted.

"I grew up in Ponce."

Marisol's voice startled me, and I turned. She was leaning against the stone wall. Her fingers were lifted to her throat, where she was twirling a gold charm. It glinted twice in the moonlight. The rest of her was in shadow.

"My mom moved me and my little sister out here last May. I don't know if Ruben told you that or not." She shrugged. "I like it here, I guess."

Marisol dropped her charm as I approached her. I put my hand on her waist and felt the soft flesh under her dress give into my slight pressure. With my free hand, I brushed a strand of her hair away from her face and then ran my fingertips over one of the straps of her dress.

"So," I whispered, "you've been waiting for me?"

Marisol didn't even let the last word leave my lips before she grabbed the sides of my face and pulled my mouth to hers. Our rum-soaked lips collided and slid against each other's. Her hands were frantic and everywhere: in my hair, on my stomach, up the front of my T-shirt. I gasped as she raked her nails across the skin of my chest. When I threw my hands to the wall behind her to brace myself, she pressed her hips into mine and ran her teeth along the edge of my jaw.

I reeled back, needing a second to catch my breath.

Marisol's dark eyes were shimmering from the liquor and the moonlight, but I only caught a glimpse of them before she came crashing down on me again.

It was only seconds later, as I was grasping for the hem of Marisol's dress, when I felt something small and sharp run across my cheek. I thought it was one of Marisol's nails, until I realized her fingers were tugging at my belt loops. Something else pelted me on the shoulder, another on the top of my head.

I made the mistake of glancing up and was struck twice in quick succession, once in the center of my forehead and then again in the tender spot between my eyebrow and eye. Marisol shrieked and dodged away. I ducked and covered my head just as several tiny pellets showered down on me.

And then, everything was quiet. I knelt down, picked up a

couple of the projectiles from around my feet, and rolled them around in my palm. They were stones, rough-edged and the size of small marbles.

I hurled them back up to their source and shouted. "Hey!" The stones came up short and rattled back down the wall. "Who's up there?"

I craned my head and was just able to make out the dark shapes of leaves swaying against a dark sky. Behind those leaves was something else, shadowed and stationary. There was a rustling noise, but that could've been from anything: the wind, a bird, a cat chasing a bird.

"That house is cursed," Marisol said, her voice slurred.

I lowered my gaze and gaped at her. She was still leaning against the stones. A strap of her dress had slipped down and was hanging loosely around her upper arm. Much of her dark hair had fallen like a curtain in front of her face, and neither of us made an effort to sweep it back.

"That house is *cursed*," she said louder, as if I didn't hear her the first time. "That's what everyone says. Didn't you know that?" She swayed to the side and let out a short burst of laughter.